What Jamie Did Next

What Jamie Did Next

David Grant

This edition 2024
Refreshing Words Press
www.refreshingwords.co.uk

ISBN 978-1-7392350-2-4

A catalogue reference for this book is available from the British Library.

Cover and book design by Paul Fulton
Cover Photograph: Unsplash/Donna White

To everyone who raved about Elephant all those years back – thank you. Hope you enjoy this one. You know who you are.

Thanks to Paul Fulton for his patience, hard work, and friendship.

'If my thought-dreams could be seen
They'd probably put my head in a guillotine ...'

Spring 2008

1. Watching the River Flow

The alarm clock shrieks inches from my ear. This time it has awakened me. I glance at it remembering that I had set it last night – Sunday – for 9.30 am.

9.30 am? I hear you ask, on a Monday morning? Whatever is the matter? Why is our dear Jamie Gallagher, captain of industry, publishing (or as we call it now 'content') magnate not awake hours sooner? Why is he not battling for his place on the 7.15 with all those other sad fucks from the City in their handmade suits and political views from the 1950s? Could it be a bank holiday? Might Jamie be poorly?

Oh no, you think. Has Jamie, consummate bullshitter, finally been found out and fired? Is this new indolence the result of recent, but not entirely unexpected, unemployment? Has the alarm gone off thus simply to give our hero the chance to wash his oxters prior to a meeting at the DHSS or whatever the fuck the dole people have been rebranded as now?

Well Dear Reader, thank you sincerely for your concern. No really. It's greatly appreciated. And I know in the past I have lavished the self-deprecation on you, my only friend, and so you would be right to consider incompetence or incontinence the most likely cause of my tardiness.

But you'd be wrong

And let me tell you why.

Think back to when last we met. My formerly trophy, now atrophied, missus had run off with Edward, he of the reinsurance empire. My trip around the UK, my various brushes with unfaithfulness rendered inconsequential compared to what I had now become – a happy, nay delighted, cuckold. Hip hip fucking hooray, I sang as I left the two of them together – he looking slightly startled as to what had happened, she looking for all the world as if she already knew she was making a big mistake. I was free. I was out of there. I even began seeing eye to eye with the children again: laughing, joking, spending quality time with them outside of the house, away from the prole-shit TV that seemed to constantly drone on in the background of my previous life.

I came back from my round Britain quest able to analyse quite how I had become such a miserable, fat, cynical perma-pissed shit-head. Well, maybe I didn't really discover why as such, but I did have some satisfaction in finding out that just about everyone I had ever known was in the same – if not worse – position than me. I was not the freak, I was one in amongst a whole shoal, flock or school of (what is the collective noun I'm looking for here?) freaks. I, through a process of self-discovery and self-diagnosis, had come through it all with flying colours.

And I had been offered the job from heaven. More money than I knew what to do with –given my ex-wife could no longer legitimately mug me for earnings. Apparently, she now had an account at Harvey Nicks, something that somehow I had always managed to avoid. Poor Edward I mused. I wonder if you could get insured against that.

I worked hard. I focused, I stopped questioning everything about the life I was leading and just frankly got fucking well on with it. I wasn't a windswept poet, or indeed any sort of poet. I didn't live in the North, I wasn't teaching talented but disadvantaged kids to express themselves through the medium of tap dance. I was me. I had made my choices early on: to follow this life of business and responsibility and an existence in the crowded, twat-infested, South East of England – commuting, worrying about profit margin and how to play the political games that one has to master to succeed in Big Business.

I hope I don't disappoint you, Dear Friend, with such a display of cynicism. Don't see it as such, please. Don't think ill of me. It's harsh reality I am afraid. It's what happens. OK, inside of me there still beats the heart of an existentialist philosopher/trawlerman/pantyhose designer, – or possibly a giddy combination of all three (what a fantastic South Bank Special that would have made, eh Mr Bragg?). But I have accepted my lot.

Why? Because it's the world I know as an adult. Because I don't want to live in a croft. I quite like having a comfortable car. I rather like being quite good at my job (God knows how – it just shows the criminal levels of incompetence amongst every other fucker in this business). And of course I have two children who, maybe naively I believe, need a father around to restrict just how screwed up they become as adults.

Self-justification over, you will be mightily relieved to hear.

Business went well. We hit our numbers. We set up an online content company that exceeded all expectation and for which I rather luckily got the credit. So, while our competitors were sitting scratching their arses bemoaning the state of the economy and struggling to keep up with the digital world, we were flying. The American masters were delighted, they gave me chunks of export markets to sprinkle my gold dust over, which I duly did, enjoying business class travel to exotic climes.

And then Johnnie hit the big time.

I had been at school with Johnnie and he had been a mad bastard then. He was expelled at sixteen. We were never really close mates in those days, but when I found him on Oldpals.com I was intrigued. I remember classrooms of uncontrollable laughter when Johnnie acted up. My favourite were French lessons, when he would reply for no explicable reason and completely deadpan to 'Comment vous-appelez vous?' with 'Je m'appelle Hughie Green'. When I was doing my Round Britain Tour of every miserable screwed up fuck I had ever met, I had included him.

We'd met in the café of the Royal Scottish Museum, surrounded by Yummy Morningside Mummies with their ridiculously named, twenty-years-away-from-jobs-in-the-bank offspring all having simultaneous tantrums. Johnnie had turned up looking for all the world like he had stepped out of the front cover of Tramp and Hobo Monthly. Long, greasy hair, a beard that had enough food attached he could have played Mr Twit in the West End, clothes so dirt-incrusted that I suspect the museum staff burnt the chair he had been sitting on the moment we'd departed.

Now, Johnnie had a passion – no, not for park benches, cider and baked hedgehog. It was for the ancient world. He was mad for the literature of the Romans and spent his life translating the works of Plautus, Terence, Catullus, Virgil and Ovid and putting them in contemporary settings.

Complete fucking lunacy of course, I had been rather struck by his passion. It resonated for me in the light of the passionless world I was living in at the time, and I gave him a contract for four of these works. The usual deal in these cash-strapped times (unless you're a breast-enhanced kiss and tell supermodel married to a professional footballer whose IQ is displayed on the back of his shirt) is to receive a tiny advance but a huge upside on the royalties when the book hits thirty thousand units. Which of course, these never would and Jimmy didn't care anyway. He was doing it for love, for the thrill of seeing his life's work in print.

Then a TV production company made an enquiry. They were interested in a six parter of the Aeneid. It happened: we repackaged the book as a TV tie-in and sold a hundred thousand copies around the world as the programme was sold to some twenty countries. They snapped up Plautus, Terence and ther est, and suddenly we had hot, hot property. Jimmy's first royalty payment was enough for him to put a fifty per cent deposit down on a flat in the New Town.

Hollywood bought the rights.

Bastard still owes me the hundred quid I lent him the day we met, but it now seems churlish to remind him.

I was hailed as the most prescient publisher of the moment who had single-handedly reintroduced the Classics to the masses.

My salary increased, as did those share options that I had barely paid any attention to when I started working for the business.

In two short years, they were worth millions. Literally.

Then a takeover war ensued as a major US media conglomerate decided they had to buy us. I sat for a period of months as rumours flew about valuations. I could never bring myself to believe that any of this was going to happen. That Jamie Gallagher could soon be a wealthy fellow.

It did happen.

I am indeed a wealthy fellow. How much wealth do I have? Well, I shall not divulge that – to do so would be vulgar. And anyway, it's all relative. Compared to someone doing well in (just as an example) reinsurance, I've copped a few years of bonus and salary in a nice lump sum. Compared to a hedge fund owner, I am a pauper – my wealth being just a couple of year's worth of donations to the Tory party to ensure a knighthood. But unless I do something very silly, I have enough money to live comfortably for the rest of my life and see the children are OK.

The Americans had wanted me on a three year earnout. I told them to fuck off. I said six months. We agreed a year. I am a non-exec director for them for two days a month for which I am paid royally and frankly intend to do absolutely sod all for, as by the time they notice I will have resigned.

Now, Dear Reader, to cut a seemingly very long story short, today is the first day for me of freedom. Hence the alarm clock, the lie in, the feeling of mild elation.

So what does Jamie do next?

I lie in the bed for ten more minutes wondering precisely that. I get up, make a cup of tea, come back to bed and continue to ponder once more on the day ahead.

I must get the papers delivered. It will be nice to lie in bed and read, drink tea, read the news, I muse. I have never liked a TV in my bedroom. There's something just a little council flat-ish about households that have a TV in every room, including the bog.

I get up and ablute. I am feeling good.

One thing you should know, old friend, is that I – Jamie, he who single-handedly kept both the distillers of Speyside and the viticulturist of Piedmont and Bordeaux in ass's milk over the last few years, paid for their children's education and second homes – have sobered up.

In the last year, I made some rules: 1) No booze Monday–Friday, except if a) abroad b) faced with a lunch/dinner of such appalling tedium that it was a straightforward toss up between alcohol and insanity; and 2) no drinking on my own. Ever. Consequently, I have lost a couple of stone and God knows I needed to do that. I sleep deeply without the pressure to wake at four am, to visit the toilet – thus putting what remains of the inshore fishing fleet in the south of England in deep, deep peril. People tell me I look years younger. The red boozer's cheeks and accessorised nose have all but gone. My teeth are no longer stained by red wine and fags. Yes, the fags have gone, too. Never even tempted.

So you find me in the rudest of health. I have just joined a trendy – now don't laugh –gym.

There may be ulterior motives for that, I confess.

I get up after half an hour of further light slumber, draw back the blinds in the living room and note that, for early May, the sun is indeed shining brightly. I pick up the remains of last night's supper

– a cup and plate – and take them through to the kitchen. Not a wine glass to be seen

I like this flat, I muse. When Helen and I split, I moved here. It was the first place I saw, it was just about in my then price range, and it was in the centre of town near to the pubs and restaurants that I envisaged using in my solitary bachelorhood. It had a spare bedroom so the kids could stay if they so wished, it was low maintenance, reasonably soundproofed and quite light and airy.

Despite the change in my circumstances, I no longer own property. I could virtually buy this entire block now if I wanted to but to be renting somehow makes me feel free, young and slightly unconventional. Stupid, I know, pouring money down a landlord's throat monthly with nothing coming back for it.

But fear ye not – rest assured, I am a happy bunny doing so.

I make a cup of coffee and out of curiosity I switch on the television. I have heard tell of the horrors of daytime TV, but have rarely ever experienced it for myself. It's not boredom driving me to do this – of course not, perish the thought. I can't be bored in the very first days of freedom. I can't imagine Mandela, his first morning out of Ellis Island, asking Winnie if she'd switch on Boer Supermarket Sweepstake as he was at a loose end. No, this is part of the beginnings of my new life, it's something I have to experience for myself, just to acclimatise.

There's a programme on there featuring a fat bloke and his breasts-hanging-out-for-all-the-world-to-see wife who have made their fortune in pies in Wigan (or something somewhere similar) and who now want to move to Spain. The Spanish are welcome to them I think switching channels. The Moors obviously fucked off due to clairvoyancy.

Kids cartoons and adverts. I flick. Ah – here we are.

I've come in halfway through a reality confessional TV show – I have heard talk of such things. There's a lot of shouting. A woman in leisurewear too awful even for Maidstone Town Centre, is pregnant and crying. Oh and about eighteen stone and hideous. There are two blokes being restrained by shave-headed bouncer types as they are obviously determined to beat the shit out of each other for the cameras. The smug middle-class presenter tells me that they're going to calm things down while they go for a commercial break.

I'm mesmerised as I sit through adverts for debt-consolidation businesses, Pot Noodle, online bingo, and celeb magazines. What targeted advertising.

Soon they're back on and I listen fascinated as Fat Woman tells Dim Boy 1 (shaven-headed, large fake diamond earrings, tattoo and all the native intelligence of a red mullet on the fish stall at Tesco) that it was very likely her daughter – their daughter – had indeed been fathered by Dim Boy 2, who was very similar to Dim Boy 1 on account of they being brothers. Apparently when DB1 was on remand for theft then DB2 would pop round for a little TLC.

There's a fight brewing again as the two Dim Boys start swearing (thankfully bleeped out for the delicate ears of the audience) at each other and threatening to slit throats, kill, maim etc.

And then the twist. I kind of knew that this programme needed some extra piquancy to keep it going for the next fifteen minutes, and so I was anticipating a further denouement. And by jingo we've got it.

On walks George. George looks early fifties. Earringed, tattooed, shaven-headed. He's wearing a vest as you so obviously do on national TV – what were you thinking of Mr Dimbleby? – that shows big arms and much greying chest hair. He's short, squat, muscular and looks like a psychopathic armed robber.

Turns out he is a psychopathic armed robber. And the father of DBs 1 and 2. Oh, and in a brief window when DB1 was on remand and DB2 was hiding up in Carlisle because he'd been a bit naughty to a local villain, daddy had come out of prison after a ten-year stretch and found his son's partner rather accommodating. From At Her Majesty's to his daughter-in-law's pleasure, indeed.

There's mayhem in the studio as the credits roll and I am absolutely hooked. I wonder if the poor daughter has to buy three Father's Day cards every year just to cover all the bases.

What is it with these people that they want to parade their semen-splashed dirty laundry on national television? It's appalling, fascinating, revolting and utterly marvellous.

I shake my head in mild desperation at the ways of the world and decide to take advantage of the sunshine. I shall venture out.

2. Perfect Skin

Washed, shaved and dressed I leave the flat. I have a plan. I shall walk to a pub on the outskirts of town that serves good food and wine. Yes, I know, I don't drink during the week or on my own, but today feels like a day of celebration and frankly I can do what the fuck I like.

The first part of the journey takes me through the shopping centre. I am not a shopper, I rarely visit this place unless absolute necessity demands that I do. Down to my last pair of clean underpants, that kind of necessity. And I never normally visit midweek.

It's busy. There are young mothers: some yummy, some less so, everywhere. The town is socially divided. Middle and upper-middle-class mothers, husbands toiling in the City contemplating affairs that will eventually break up their marriages – push babies in designer buggies which cost as much as a small car, while shopping casually and meeting their friends for coffee or lunch. And then the fun starts – the gossiping, the boasting, the leaving-the-car-keys-of-the-new-Porsche on the table accidentally so everyone notices and comments. The Caribbean fortnight this summer, the Paris surprise for the wedding anniversary (that actually was assuaging the husband's guilt for shagging his secretary rather poorly at that conference in Frankfurt a couple of weeks back).

The less yummy are but kids – anything from fourteen to seventeen-year-old girls who should still be in school, but who are suffering for accommodating their condomless, now absent, boyfriends. It's leisur wear, hooped earrings, gum, pouty lips and false eyelashes, swearing and chewing with midriffs on view. Strangely the buggies that their children are pushed around in are virtually identical or superior to those of the yummy mummies. Presumably bought from The Catalogue and paid for monthly out their benefits.

Which my fucking taxes are paying for. Makes my blood boil. Get a fucking job. Or put something in the water to stop their fertility. What has happened to personal responsibility? Everything is everyone else's fault. You get up the duff in the park at fifteen after too many alcopops and the state will care for you.

Makes my blood boil.

And also scares me to think I am capable of such a middle-class, middle-aged Victorian- values inner rant. What has happened to me? What is happening to the man more Liberal in his views than Gladstone himself, who believed in the empowerment of the

Working Classes (although he wouldn't want to share a lift with any of them), who believed in Society helping the unfortunates?

I remember as a young man at university briefly toying with the idea of teaching. I wanted to promulgate knowledge. To work with working-class kids brought up on *The Generation Game* and *Little and Large* so that they would weep at *Lear* and *Othello*, love Austen and the Brontës and melt and understand the power of the twentieth-century novel by devouring Greene.

OK so my career path changed when I realised how shit the money was, but the passion for equality was always there. I marched for the miners, I demonstrated against Thatcher, I read *The Guardian*, and not just the sports pages.

Now my views seem to have become so right wing I'd be deemed too extreme for the letters page of the *Daily Mail*.

I pass the recently opened Ann Summers shop and think how different the world is today. Dildos on the high street. Sex everywhere. A bloke of my age has to be careful when the weather turns. There's so much flesh on display you can easily face accusations of being a dirty old man, when girls young enough to be my daughter walk around town centres as if they've just popped off the beach in Ibiza. I have a rule in these situations, despite my innate ability to ogle (particular penchant for bosoms I have to confess), it's eyes ahead, don't fall for the obvious and keep yourself out of trouble.

I am ascending on the escalator. Halfway up in front of me I cannot help but notice a blond woman in tight jeans with a bottom to die for. I stare safe in the knowledge that I cannot be found out unless she turns round.

She walks off the escalator and I follow, only because I am genuinely going in that direction, still staring at her backside... when suddenly she does turn around. She's obviously remembered something. I feel immediately guilty, caught mid-lech, then I feel confused.

It's Helen. My ex-wife Helen. She looks at me and smiles. I have been ogling my ex. Yuck, that's kind of unnatural. A sort of incest, surely?

I haven't seen her for a couple of months, but something has happened to her. She looks ... transformed. Ten years younger, beautiful once more. She sees me and smiles. I walk towards her and kiss her on both cheeks. 'God,' I say 'You look fantastic Helen. What's happened?'

'Meaning I never used to, Jamie?' she says and smiles. She looks like the girl I met some twenty-odd years back in London.

'You look ... different. Younger. Sorry, Helen, I'm just a little... stunned.'

'It's nice I can still stun you, James Gallagher,' she says slightly coquettishly, I think ...

'Oh,' she says as she looks me up and down, 'you look pretty good yourself'.

Is she flirting with me?

We chat a little then she says, 'If you buy me a coffee, I'll tell you my secret.'

It seems churlish to refuse and we plump for one of the 563 fair trade maestro barista establishments within two hundred metres of where we are standing.

We get our coffees and sit. She tells me her secret.

It's not much of a secret. She had felt that she'd let herself go a little, started taking Edward somewhat for granted. So, she'd employed a personal trainer and dietician. She started feeling better, then treated herself to a week in Poland. At a plastic surgeon's clinic. New arse, tummy tuck and she said seductively, of that I am certain, 'New boobs,' as she pushed them out towards me. 'So, what do you think?'

'Lovely,' I say, uncertain how to respond to a flirtatious ex-wife and desperately trying not to ogle. 'But more importantly, what does Edward think?'

'Oh, he's thrilled. Dear old stick. When he remembers to look.' And she gave me a strange sideways glance which is nothing if not bordering on the seductive.

Oh, I get it, I think. Oh, I really get it. She knows. Somehow she knows about the money. I go a little cold, both at my terrible cynicism but also at the thought that Helen might be being duplicitous in some way.

'So how are you then Jamie? How is life? How is the Corporation?'

'It's fine,' I say, non-committedly.

'Still in the flat?'

'Yup.' She knows all this. She's fishing.

'Not working today?'

'Day off,' I say.

'I heard,' here it comes I think, as she smiles at me just a little seductively, 'that you'd had a pay out?'

'Helen,' I say, sighing, disappointed in myself for being flattered by the superficial attraction and indeed the resulting excitement, 'the divorce settlement is done and dusted. There's nothing more there. I maintain the kids, as agreed. You've no more claims on me, I'm afraid.' I bristle a little as I sip my coffee

She looks hurt. 'Darling, I'm not after anything more from you. I just hope you're enjoying your success. You deserve it.' She smiles sweetly then in turn sips her coffee.

I am, at heart, a cynical, deeply flawed bastard, I think. She means it. She's happy for me.

I know what the problem is really here. I am finding her attractive, still. Very attractive. The top two buttons of her blouse have opened *comme magique* and there's not a little cleavage on show. Oh, and it's firm cleavage. And despite myself, knowing this way be dragons, I take a glance.

Trouserly stirrings.

She catches me looking. I feel as if I have been apprehended riffling through an elderly aunt's knicker drawer.

'Take me for lunch, darling,' she says, naming the most expensive and frankly overrated restaurant in town.

'I can't,' I say quickly. 'I have business to attend to.'

I drink my coffee and tell her I have to go. 'Tomorrow night,' she says, as I stand up to leave, 'I shall be in George's. Meet me there at eight.'

'OK,' I say if only to get rid of her. I'll phone and cancel later but I just have to get away from her and that cleavage. Now.

I kiss her on cheeks and virtually run from the coffee house.

Fuck fuck fuck fuck and indeed thrice fuck I think as I walk away and head out of town. Oh, and bollocks.

3. What Made Milwaukee Famous

Well let me give you a little lesson in success, Dear Friend.

Let me share with you a little glimpse of what goes on inside the mind of a fabulously successful creative bloke like me.

I'm in the pub, obviously. I needed shelter and sustenance after my morning walk in the valley of death with my ex-missus. Thinking time. Space.

Five pints of strong ale and a couple of cigars later, you find me having sorted out this potentially messy problem. I have analysed the facts, I have worked out what the issues are here.

I have another beer whilst I put the finishing touches to my theory.

Fact 1 – I have, in the four years since Helen and I split, not had a significant other. I've worked too hard. There have been a couple of near things, a casual grope and snog with a New York colleague in a hotel lift after a long flight and a boozy meal – but in terms of actual penetrative let's-swap-some-good-old-fashioned-bodily-fluids sex, forget it. I have not been interested in the involvement, and involvement there would have been, in that I don't really do casual intercourse terribly well. Also I have never been able to multi-task effectively, and I wasn't going to put myself off my game whilst building my empire and so I resolutely kept my somewhat neglected knob out of my day-to-day life.

Fact 2 – Helen must know something of my new financial situation. There were press releases about the various stages of the sale and my subsequent employment, and she probably could work out with Edward, who is many things but being financially dim-witted isn't one of them, the kind of figure I ended up with.

Fact 3 – She left me originally through (in no particular order) a) my mild mid-life crisis; b) Edward's superior financial situation; c) my frankly boorish, constantly pissed, dissatisfied-with-my-lot atrocious behaviour. And frankly, in retrospect, who could blame her?

Fact 4 – She saw a father figure in Edward, who would look after her financially. Obviously, she could not ever, *ever* have found Edward – or indeed any bloke – more attractive than me and so it was *sans doute* the money motive only that made her walk.

The break-up didn't bother me, truly. I was not hurt, distraught, or in any way pained at her unfaithfulness. We'd run our course. The mediocrity of my marriage to Helen was now replaced in my mind by the mediocrity of her marriage to that boring old fuck Edward. If anything, I felt sorry for them.

The settlement had been very fair. I willingly agreed to support the children and to pay education costs. Helen went off and lived with Edward in their moated house. The kids lived there but visited me virtually every weekend and royally took the piss, much to my delight, out of Edward and his fuddy-duddy ways. Cameron is now on a gap year which I suspect might turn into a gap decade as he's having fun travelling and Ailsa is mid A levels planning a gap year. They receive from me the financial support I originally committed to.

No way the children will or need to know of their father's wealth. What would motivate them to get out of bed in the morning if they know they're virtually set for life? Absolutely bugger all. So, it's student loans for the both of them, a need to accept personal financial responsibilities during university life, and I'll settle their debts when they've graduated. But they've not been told that, at least by me.

It's all worked out. I will not be responsible for making my children spoilt brats. Helen must not be allowed to mess this grand plan up by telling them of my situation.

That's that decided. I have another drink. I'll worry about cancelling her tomorrow.

I think about my future. It might, just might, get a little lonely. Now I've always enjoyed my own company, there's none better in my humble opinion. But for the next thirty (God willing) years? Should I start to look for someone with whom to grow old?

I've avoided it, not needing the involvement, too busy. Also, there's something slightly repulsive about the language that is used when folk of a certain age go looking for a partner. It's all so borrowed from teenagers. To hear middle-aged people talk about dating, their boyfriend/girlfriend, it's just so ... unseemly. Perhaps this is a throwback to my Scottish Presbyterian upbringing where, as previously discussed, your parents acted as parents not as slightly older siblings and fucking behaved themselves.

A couple of people have suggested internet or speed dating. Yuck. Humiliation obviously lies down that route. I have had no real interest in any of the women who I have worked with except, of course, for darling Janice – my former receptionist who I poached and made my PA. She was without doubt the least effective PA in the history of that particular function, but her smile, tight sweaters and firm calves made my days even more bearable. But that was never going to be anything more than mild office flirting on her part and lust on mine. You'll probably struggle to believe me but I would never have dreamt of overstepping the boss/employee line.

Too open to understandable accusations of male exploitation.

Why this self-analysis? It's fucking obvious why. If you'd just been hit on by your ex-wife who has defrosted your gonads by flashing her Polish breasts and you'd liked it – you wouldn't feel the need to ask that question. I was immensely flattered by her attentions and, let's be honest, tempted at least to consider cuckolding Mr Reinsurance in the same way he had cuckolded me.

No, I tell myself, finishing the beer and paying the tab. No. No. Ain't going to happen.

I start to walk back towards town. I feel disappointed about how the day has panned out. My first day of liberation has soured in a fit of over-libation.

Put simply, as I am nothing if not a simple fellow, I thought my life was sorted out. It fucking isn't.

The outskirts of town where the industrial estates are situated, are reminiscent of a mediaeval city. In those days you'd have the furriers or candle-makers together in one street. Now you've the electrical and plumbing suppliers, the DIY superstores, the car dealers all in similar enclaves.

I walk past the Mercedes dealership and stop. There's a car on the forecourt ...

I think I've fallen in love. I stare. It's a lot of money for a car. But it's beautiful, a small black compact-designed convertible sports car.

I stare.

I have a nice car already, I think, my big BMW. I don't need another car. And not a sports car, not at my age. What do they say about sports cars and middle-aged blokes? Oh yes, I remember. They are bought by rich middle-aged blokes chasing their youth and compensating for their slackening libido.

I walk past the little piece of tarty Germanic engineering, determined not to fall for its sleek seductive lines.

But I could just go in and enquire. Ask for a brochure. Where would the harm be in that?

I walk into the glistening reception area and approach a pretty dark-haired girl behind the desk. She looks me up and down and asks, not very convincingly, if she can help me.

I can see her point. I have just walked a couple of miles in spring sunshine after consuming beer and cigars that she could probably smell off me from before I entered the premises. I've just walked in to this establishment. My shirt is hanging out and I'm rather sweaty. Astutely, she has me identified as a pissed tramp.

'That black sports car out front – I'd like some details please.'

'With a view to ... ?' she asks.

'Buying the bloody thing, actually,' I say a little aggressively then change my tack. 'Did you think perhaps I wanted permission to sketch it in charcoal on your forecourt?' I smile at my humorous invention.

She bristles, picks up the phone on the desk behind her and obviously says rather more to the colleague at the other end of the line than just, 'You've a customer.'

'Take a seat, sir, ' that last word uttered almost venomously, she says. 'Someone will be with you shortly.'

'Shall I help myself to coffee?' I say nodding at a machine and cups and saucers.

She ignores me. I pour a cup of black coffee and sit down. I pick up the *Daily Mail*. It's enough to make you walk out.

'Sir,' says a snappily besuited young man of about fifteen. 'How can we help you today?'

I tell him about the black car on the forecourt. He mentions a name for it that sounds like a chemical compound that might cure eczema.

'It is expensive sir. Seventy-five thousand'.

'I noticed that. Tell me what it does please.' He sighs, looking me up and down. In a bored voice he tells me about horsepower and torque and pistons and I stop him. 'Sorry Mr ...?' He offers his name, Peter. 'Peter, I don't want to be rude, but I know nothing about cars. Just tell me basics. Top speed? Automatic? How many seats? Servicing? Miles per hour?'

He tells me all of this still in a bored voice.

'Thank you,' I say. 'Now, if I pay cash is there a discount?'

He is looking at me thinking he's been had. 'Cash? Seventy five grand? Come on sir, you're taking the piss. You've obviously had a few too many and you're having a great joke. It's gone far enough now. I have to ask you to leave.'

'OK Peter,' I say affably. 'You're right. I don't have that kind of money on me obviously. Sorry to mislead you.'

'That's OK ... Sir,"' he says wearily shepherding me to the door. I shake his hand. Reaching for my wallet, I take out my Platinum Amex card and hold it up to him.

'You my young friend, should learn not to be judgemental.'

My somewhat tumultuous first day of my new life was made somewhat better by the purchase of the beautiful, black sporty Merc. For £65k. Pick it up on Friday.

I walk back through the town centre. Via the off-licence. I revisit my vow of abstinence and remember a caveat.

It only applied to Speyside Scotch.

I treat myself to a bottle of Islay's finest and return to the flat.

4. Sugar on my Tongue

The alarm clock shrieks in my ear but this time it has not woken me up.

I have been awake with the symptoms of the bad old days. A rumbling in my guts reminiscent of the key special effects in *Krakatoa East of Java* started it all off at four am. Then the headache kicked in about the same time as the heady cocktail of worry, self-doubt, disbelief, revulsion and self-loathing rose within me like some perfect soufflé of absolute abject fucking misery.

What have I done? What the bleeding fucking bastarding fuck have I fucking done?

First off, after two years of rational behaviour vis-à-vis the plonk, I have on my first day on civvy street gone out and got absolutely wasted. Oh yes, Dear Friend, I should tell you that my evening did not stop at Scotch. I popped back out to the offie at 9.30 pm as I convinced myself that I now had a medical condition, excessive Scotch induced heartburn, that could only – no, really – only be cured by a bottle of Barolo. And of course, my monk-like vow of abstinence did not apply to wine of any sort when imbibed as part of medical necessity – as it would undoubtedly be in this situation. I could freelance for the *Lancet*, me.

Of course, I bought two bottles. Silly not to. Left half of one I believe. And half the Scotch. That must be why my mouth resembles a Bedouin's jock strap.

That ... and the packet of Marlboro Light I bought and consumed alongside the wine.

So, what else should trouble me as the dawn chorus irritatingly kicks off outside, apart from a return to my destructive addictions of old?

Oh yes, I remember now. There was the unbridled gusset straining trouserly tumescence brought on by my ex-wife's new body. And how I had dribbled over her cleavage like a diabetic over a sweet trolley. And she caught me staring. And I'm supposed to be taking her out for dinner this evening.

Fuckety fuck fuck fuck.

Krakatoa erupts and I head for the barely adequate facilities of the flat.

And another thing troubles me. Someone once told me that Krakatoa was actually *west* of Java, but that the filmmakers thought *east* sounded better so the geographical vérité was crumpled up and discarded.

I know I will need to check this out on the internet. Soon. Or it will bother me.

But there's still something further looming at the back of mind about yesterday – something quite big and rather troublesome that part of my psyche is trying to protect me from.

Oh yes, fuck me. I just spent – when pissed – sixty-five thousand pounds on a car I've never even driven because I wanted to show a pre-pubescent car salesman what a big rich bastard I was. Pure petulance.

OK, I can afford it. By a long way. But that degree of flashiness is not me, that's not the lad from Edinburgh whose proudest automotive experience to date was taking delivery of my very first company car in 1982. A red Sierra. With radio.

And what if I have an irresistible compulsion to go out daily from now on, get pissed and buy a car just because some spotty twat irritates me?

A quick calculation. I can't do the compound interest bit in my head but in rough terms if I repeated yesterday's outing just one hundred times – that's a little over three months, I will be skint once more. A sobering thought.

I complete the life and death struggle that is my battle with the lavatory (I think the lavatory wins, by the way) and head for the kitchen. Tea is what I need now

I go back to bed, hoping to drift back off, but I can't. The weight of my worries hangs heavy.

OK, I take them one by one.

The precise Krakatoa-location issue probably isn't important right now, so I'll park that.

The booze and fags – yup, they are a worry. My behaviour suggests long-standing addiction that my recent self-control had only kept in check, never cured. I have a problem. I cannot allow myself to slip back to earlier ways of behaviour, or else I shall be unhappy and alone. And probably dead.

Conclusion? Immediate detox. Throw the remains of the booze down the sink and chuck the remaining five – how could I have smoked fifteen for Christ's sake? – fags away. Then go to the poncy gym for the morning and sweat all the bad stuff out of me. Work out hard, maybe do a class, go to the steam-room, swim, and take a sauna until every last drop of crap has been forced screaming through my pores.

And revisit the vows – removing the recently added codicil so that all alcohol and tobacco, no matter its almost magical medical properties, or indeed provenance, be included.

Easy. Sorted.

The car. Sleep on it. Where's the harm? I've got the money, it was rather lovely, I deserve to treat myself. I can sell the Beamer if my guilt deems it necessary.

Then that just leaves the issue of Helen.

As her name pops in to my head I get a vision of her pert backside and smooth expanse of breast and oh fuck me no – before I know it, the middle of the duvet is doing a passable impression (not to scale, obviously) of Krakatoa – east or west of Java I currently know not which, due to pyjamaly stirrings.

This reaction needs attention. It is not natural. You divorced this woman because you could not stand to be in the same house as her, with her middle-class shopping orgies, dull friends with ponytails and their fuckwit dull, financier husbands. You rejoiced when you found out she was having her policies renewed on a regular basis with Edward. You were the happiest fellow alive.

Now this. She can't have changed in any way but physically - and even with her new body she's not exactly Jenny Agutter in the shower scene in *American Werewolf in London* (sometimes I just so age myself). I've had better looking, firmer and younger women giving me the eye of late as my power grew and my waistline shrank. Trust me I have. And yet no stirrings occurred in any way to rival the seismic penile force currently trying to bust my PJs.

I need to be rational.

I get my *Sunday Times Atlas of the World* out (look, I am a book man, me, OK?). Bugger me. Krakatoa is indeed west of Java.

How can that be?

Phew, tumescence alarm can now be switched off. I sit at the kitchen table with another mug of tea and try to work out, rationally, my attraction to a woman who until yesterday lived in my memory as a money-grabbing somewhat vapid member of the genus Hirudinea (alright, we published the definitive guide to them that's how I know ...).

OK, thinking back to when I first met her, in the late eighties in London. She was a temp, I was in my first management job. She had blond hair and a sense of fashion that mixed the fading new-romanticism of the age, with a bouquet of post-punk and a soupçon of hippy. A unique look. Breasts then to die for, and a smile that enticed, as I asked her to file or photocopy or whatever PAs were meant to do in those days.

They were sociable times. Unlike today no one batted an eyelid if half the company went to the pub on a Friday at midday and returned at three, incoherent and incapable of serious work. As the boss of my small group of loyal followers I justified it as team-building.

Helen would join in. She'd flirt a little, flash her eyes at me, occasionally touch my arm to emphasise a point she was making to me, or chastise me for teasing someone. But that was it. Until that one night in an Irish bar in Islington and we ended up together, the rest of the team having disappeared. We drank whiskey and Guinness and I offered to walk her home and we'd kissed – but no, I couldn't come for a nightcap at her Camden flat. She wasn't that sort. And after all I was her boss ...

Remember Dim Boy 1 from the reality TV show and his red mullet impression? That was me standing outside her flat watching the light coming on in her living room and feeling so horny I could barely walk.

Certainly not to my flat in Clapham.

What was going on?

As Monday morning approached, I had become excited at the prospect of seeing her again, and anxiously planned how to address what had happened. As I sat on the bus to work I became convinced that there was something amiss. She had a secret husband or live-in lover; she was a lesbian or something; and then I thought, she's only a temp, she probably thinks I am a predatory sex fiend and she'll never show her face in the office again. Why should she? She can temp somewhere where her boss isn't constantly trying to tickle her epiglottis with his tongue.

So, by the time I had stepped off the bus, I was in a bad mood already. How dare she desert me like this, how dare she treat me with such contempt. Someone in that office would pay for the girl of my dreams walking out on me. I grunted at the receptionist with whom I usually flirted, marched stony-faced past a couple of colleagues who I'd usually have a laugh and joke with, flung open my office door throwing my briefcase heavily to the floor.

'Coffee James?' said a voice in the corner and there she was: radiant in a flowery skirt, naval jacket and bouffant blonde hair (she did dress strangely, I recall) and she smiled and I was smitten again. My anger subsided, I found excuses to be close to her.

It took me four weeks of wooing her before we made love. And it was urgent, passionate splendid lovemaking: wonderful, and deep and meaningful.

She was the one for me – I was obsessed for months.

Then things changed. Quite suddenly. Her father who was something in the City, died of a massive heart attack. Turned out the family fortune was not as sound as daddy had been pretending. Everything stopped, the family home had to be sold; the allowance that let Helen live off the paltry salary temping in a book publisher gave her, stopped too. I stood there at the funeral with Helen and felt the sea-change. She was no longer a fun-loving girl, she was a woman concerned for her future and that future was looking bleak, unless she found someone to look after her.

Of course, this was all learnt through the wisdom of hindsight. I did not realise it at the time. I thought she was just a sad young woman, upset by the misfortunes life was throwing at her, depressed, bereaved and a lot less fun that she used to be.

My interest waned. Then the thunderbolt. She was, she told me one Saturday afternoon in bed after a perfunctory bunk up, pregnant. Yup, she was certain.

Well I suggested all the options. She, a good Catholic girl told me there was only one course of action she could properly take. Two weeks later we were wed in a South London registry office, with a couple of mates as witnesses and a meal for four in the local Indian where I got pissed. Very pissed. We couldn't afford a honeymoon. We had a baby on the way and I had to provide for my family.

Provide I would 'and did, but from then the relationship was dull, punctuated by occasional bouts of lust and passion in the first ten years of marriage, when sensible alcohol intake (before insensible alcohol intake became the norm) and relaxation brought us together. But for the most part I think we both felt like we had been congenitally thrown together, joined at the hip with a twin sibling whose every action caused annoyance.

There's a job of homespun psychology to be done here, I muse, but I am too hung-over to attempt it right now.

I lie in bed thinking until that fucking alarm clock shrieks.

5. Love is the Drug

OK, this is serious. I have misbehaved. I shall punish my body this morning I decide – which I acknowledge to be the biggest miscarriage of justice since the Birmingham Six as it really should be my mind that suffers.

I shower and get changed for the gym. Old Heart of Midlothian shirt, circa 1974, few rips in it, a few stains, but it's fine. Old baggy tracksuit bottoms from around the similar time, bought I believe in the BHS sale. Mismatched socks and rather rancid late 1970s trainers.

You can take the boy out of 1970s Edinburgh but you can't take 1970s Edinburgh out of the boy. I know, I'm spending over a grand a year to be a member of this swanky gym but I absolutely refuse to go the whole hog and buy new gear. What would the point of that be? I'd spend another two hundred quid on a matching outfit just to sweat into. Fucking ridiculous. I might now have money but parsimony is no bad thing (yes, I know, that fucking car ...). My look defines me in that temple of poseurs and my look is mildly eccentric millionaire tramp. It's all about non-conspicuous wealth, about the zeitgeist of the times – which is to recycle things that are still functioning and keep them out of the landfill. So stick that in your Louis Vuitton gym bag and stick it where it'll impede the use of an exercise bike.

I put my change of clothing in a carrier bag and pop my iPod (OK, for strict recycling credibility it should be a cassette Walkman but an iPod is just so absolutely functional) and head out of the flat.

At the door I remember there is something I need to do. Phone Helen and cancel tonight. Easy. I pick my mobile up. OK granted I could go to the piss-filled call box still just about functioning at the corner of the street if I'm trying to reject all things modern – but a mobile is a necessity whereas designer T-shirts are not, if you wish to continue pushing the argument. I dial her house number. It rings six or so times then cuts to the answerphone. Edward's voice drones on. I don't leave a message – what would I say that wouldn't embarrass or implicate Helen in something painful should Edward hear it first?

I phone her mobile. It rings and rings. No messaging service. Bugger. I wanted this sorted, behind me, finished. Now, I'll have to keep trying until she eventually picks up. My day will be ruined until she does.

I drive the five miles to the gym and park. It's 9.45 and a selection of 4x4s and convertibles are in the car park already – suggesting that the gym will be awash with ladies who work out, shop, lunch then shag their gardeners. Not necessary in that order. I'll be the rogue male, the spare prick on the gynae ward. It's only the third time I've been here but I am sure I'm already marked out as the unemployed perv/drug dealer/ pornographer. I can't be a normal bloke as normal blokes are called Julian and Tarquin and sell hedge funds or whatever the fuck it is you do with a hedge fund, and they certainly don't do exercise mid-week during the day.

There are the usual fresh-faced pretty girls on reception who smile vapidly as I wave my pass at the electronic barrier. What would happen if a fat, ugly bloke applied for a job here? I mean, if he didn't get it, could he have them for discrimination against fat ugly blokes? I think I may even apply myself next time there's a vacancy. I could sit there all day and smile like a fuckwit.

Into the locker room, out again, up the stairs and I enter the gym. There are indeed about twenty women, all shapes and sizes and ages already in there. I start, as Amber my personal trainer had told me to, on the aero bike to warm up.

Fucking boring. I need some muscle-crunching sweat activity, not a fucking aero cycle, so I stay on it for just one minute before heading off to the running machine.

I take out my iPod and put the earphones in my ears. I press shuffle and start to jog gently. 'Going Down the Road Feelin' Bad' by the Grateful Dead starts up and I think I can't jog to this – so I take the iPod out of my pocket and manage to find, eventually, the forward button.

Bob Dylan singing 'Dirge' off *Planet Waves*. Again I grope for the button as the running machine is for some inexplicable reason going faster and faster and I just about stumble as I fiddle with one hand and hit forward on the iPod.

The Smiths and 'There is a Light that Never Goes Out'. Fuck I have to go with this as I know if I try to change the iPod again I am going to end up in a humiliated crumbled heap on the floor.

I run for ten minutes enjoying Roxy Music's 'Sunset' and 'Waltzing Matilda' by The Pogues.

It's like a playlist for a trainee pallbearer.

I stop when I glance in the mirror at the woman beside me and realise that compared to her I am virtually stationary.

I realise why it has taken me fifty-two years to join a gym. It's quite straightforward really, there's very little mystery in it. It's because they are terrible terrible shit places used by fucking vapid morons.

What was I thinking when I joined this fucking shithole?

Parsimony kicks in. I think of how much the joining fee set me back and then how much they mug me for monthly – and then stride resolutely towards some instrument of torture (banned by the Spanish Inquisition as too gruesome) that a petite, blond woman has just vacated. It's meant to strengthen your thighs apparently. There's an outline of a sweaty backside on the seat. Yuck. No, really, yuck . I wipe it with some paper towel, a look of disgust on my face, and then sit down, position my legs and push. Nothing. I push again. Nothing. Can't move the fucker, must be broken, you spend all that money and the machines are shit. I'll write to the owners, I think, see if I can get a rebate.

Just then Amber appears smiling beside me from nowhere. 'Try this,' she says taking off half the weight I'd inherited from she of the sweaty arse.

'That's better,' I say, although in truth it's still a couple of pounds too much for me. 'Being a bit over-ambitious,' I add and she smiles at me as one would smile at an irritating child.

I do ten or so of the exercise and my legs are screaming at me to stop or to have them amputated. I choose the former course of action, and move on to a machine that is meant to help develop my chest. That's what the diagram tells me anyhow. Of course, giving that the last user is some weak female, I take the precaution of removing three quarters of the weight before starting to use it.

I just about complete ten exercises. I then commit the cardinal sin, because I am such a pathetic out-of-condition weakling, of losing control and the weights crash against each other and everyone (no, really, everyone) in that gym – despite the cacophony of shit pop music being pumped out at high decibels – hears the clatter and stops mid pelvic floor thrust or whatever they're doing and turn around to stare at me. I try to look nonchalant as I dismount, but I do feel as though they've just seen me bare my arse on national television.

Fuck the weights, I decide. I shall use the cross-trainer. The cross-trainer is good and easy, I can control what I'm doing and I will not humiliate myself.

And that's what I do, half an hour of fairly gentle cycling listening to the news. I'm banishing the iPod for the moment until I work out how to compile a sensible playlist for gym use.

Finished in the gym, I leave with my dignity just about intact. I go downstairs, shower and prepare for my grand entrance poolside. I pull on my fluorescent swimming shorts – bought in Florida in 1992 – worst goddamn holiday I've ever been on: surrounded by clinically obese Americans called Chuck, in an alcohol-free environment in the soaking heat, pouring what little money I had then into the swelling coffers of the fucking Disney Corporation.

There, a potted history of my swimming trunks. You wouldn't get that from Ian McEwan, not about my trunks anyway, unless he's been snooping.

Anyway, I gingerly step into the shallow end. There's a kids' lesson going on so I'm restricted to the area that has been set aside for circuit swimming. Thankfully there's a fast and slow section. I choose slow and set off with my front crawl.

Six strokes in and I collide with an old lady in a flowery swimming hat. I am told in no uncertain tones to 'Watch where you're going' (by the old lady, not her swimming hat, although a talking swimming hat under these circumstances could prove to be a bit of winner). I apologise profusely, check the lane in front and set off again.

This time the collision is with a forty-something woman. 'Fucking hell,' she says. 'Can't you swim straight?'

My kinda gal. Dark hair, big brown eyes and a fabulous figure – well, from what I can tell in the split-second she's in front of me. 'I have difficulty swimming in a straight line,' I start to say but she's off, pert bottom appearing gently out of the water.

I believe I may have found my reason to come swimming.

I try to concentrate on moving through the water in a straight line. Of course I bump into the old lady again who doesn't say 'Fucking hell,' but is clearly thinking it. I know I would be if I were an old lady.

I need, I realise with sinking heart, to resort to breaststroke so at least I can see where I am fucking going. I have little enough dignity left as it is. Me trying to do breaststroke will shatter the little that remains of it, but it's that or a manslaughter charge for taking one of these women out permanently.

It's a co-ordination thing. You have to get your legs working in syncopation, your arms doing the same, and then that all happening at the same time as you stretch your feet and flatten your hands and remember to breathe and stick your head in the water and lift your head back out and it's an absolute fucking nightmare of a swimming stroke and probably should be banned on grounds that it humiliates and stigmatises uncoordinated folk like me. I achieve two lengths resembling, I believe, a kitten drowning after its central nervous system has been removed.

Fuck this for a game of marines. I head to the steam-room.

The menthol hits me immediately. There's no one else in there and so I lie flat on the top shelf of seating. I close my eyes and think that if this – not the steam-room, not the swimming pool, the whole gym thing – is meant to be pleasurable and to fill the time in my quasi-retirement, then I'd better consider some form of gainful employment again because this will drive me – to use Edinburgh vernacular – batchy.

The door clicks open and a figure slips in. It must either be the old lady or the forty-something lovely as everyone else in the pool area was with a child. I try to move gently to ascertain which through the mist, but my back has created a slight vacuum against the soaked marble of the seat and I realise my slightest movement produces a significantly loud farting noise.

Time stands still. All I can register is the purring engine that is pumping out the steam. Then a strangled laugh, from which I can guess it's the forty- not seventy-something.

'It's one of those situations,' I say to the ceiling, 'where whatever I say will seem foolish. You're sitting there thinking I've just broken wind. That, after me attempting to knock both you and that old lady out of the water. I lie up here wracked with embarrassment.' More laughter.

'So, I apologise on all fronts but in pathetic self-justification the noise you just heard was not as you imagine.'

'Apology accepted,' says the voice, 'if you will accept mine for swearing at you.'

'I won't I am afraid. You were absolutely the mistress of restraint under those circumstances, Frankly the F-word used just once fell woefully short of what the circumstances needed.'

'In that case,' said the disembodied voice, 'please accept my apology for not being even more foul-mouthed.'

'Accepted,' I say, then 'I am about to move. There may be consequences.' As I pull myself up so that I can sit properly, all hell breaks loose on the slippery fart front.

She laughs again and says 'You don't remember me, do you Jamie?'

This is getting interesting, and not a little erotic. She has a sexy, sensuous voice and from what I saw in the pool, quite a body. But I don't have a clue who she is; as far as I am concerned, I've never met her in my life before.

I have little option but to confess.

'Well to be fair,' she says 'we only did meet once. I'm Christine – a friend of Helen's. Came to your house for dinner once.'

I'm trying but still struggling.

'It was one of the funniest evenings we'd had for years. You were off your face, you and Helen were at each other's throats.'

'That narrows it down to virtually any evening in sixteen years of marriage,' I interrupt.

'And you had a bit of an argument with Mike, I recall.'

'Mike?' I say. Something is coming to back to me.

'Mike. My husband. Or rather my then husband.'

I remember now. 'Twas not dear Jamie's finest hour, I recollect. I was half way through my second bottle of Chablis by the time they arrived. She was very pretty, had tight jeans and a lovely figure. He was clean-cut, an Oxford Blue in virtually every sport you could name and was making a fortune in the City. Quite a nice bloke I recall, considering, until I tried a bit of one-upmanship and came several country miles a distant second. I then came up with my masterstroke which was to get wired in about a bottle of Speyside. I woke up a few hours later and they'd fucked off.

Helen had slapped me and looking back, who could blame her. What a prick I had been that night (oh and so many others, too)?

'I remember now,' I say. 'The good old days when I was at the top of my game.' She laughs at this. 'I guess I should apologise,' I say, encouraged by her laughter.

'Oh don't. It was memorable. That tension between people in those pretty horrid social situations is usually plastered over while everyone plays happy families. Your antics were quite refreshing actually, and very amusing.'

'Makes the evening sound like a Mike Leigh play'.

'There was an element of *Abigail's Party* about it, true. Only it was funnier.'

I'm impressed.

'So you and Mike ...?' I start.

'The bastard was fucking his twenty-four-year-old PA. Had been for a couple of years.'

'I'm sorry,' I say and mean it.

'Thanks but don't be. He was a smug, boring bastard anyway.'

I am liking this woman more and more.

'Buy me dinner Jamie. We can get pissed together,' she says as the door opens and the old lady appears. That puts the lid on further revealing conversations. I also realise that I have become so hot my head is about to explode. As the old lady sits down I raise myself and a rip-roaring couple of farting noises erupt. Christine stifles a laugh, the old lady says 'Well really!', I get to my feet and sway a little dizzily. I note with part alacrity, part embarrassment that there are mild trouserly stirrings that need to be disguised on exit.

'I'd love to,' I say, as I open the glass door. 'Tomorrow night. George's?'

'Eight o'clock,' she says. 'I'll see you there.'

'Cool,' I say, as I leave, trying to sound cool but feeling far from cool. I've overheated, I've been hit on by an attractive woman and so it is safe to confirm – cool I am not.

I nearly slip as I walk round the pool, towel held in front of me as tumescence-cover.

I shower. I am confused by what has just happened. I also realise that I have still to track down Helen to cancel tonight. I phone both the numbers I have for her as I walk to the car. Answerphone on the land line – I don't leave a message for reasons previously explained re Edward – and her mobile just keeps ringing.

I drive home wondering if I should move to Tibet and become a monk.

6. Both Ends Burning

I've tried tracking Helen down all bloody afternoon and I am getting not a little cross. I am tempted to leave a message at the house regardless of causing her embarrassment with Edward. Why should I care?

But I don't. That would be something of a caddish thing to do and I, Dear Friend, am many things, but not a cad.

I finish off the Barolo. I know, I was going to pour it down the sink, but it would have been criminal to have done so – considering how much it cost me and anyhow, this is for medicinal purposes once more. My heart is beating so hard and fast with anxiety about the coming evening that the wine is a necessity.

And somehow, I forgot to chuck the Marlboros away, and so I have a couple of those in the kitchen as I drink my wine and think. I try her mobile again and there's no answer. I wait ten minutes before trying once more. No answer. A thought occurs. I have a slug of wine and dig out my address book. I must have made a mistake entering her number on my phone's memory. So I dial the number from the address book and as it rings the screen tells me I'm calling Helen Mob. So I have had the right number all along but she isn't answering.

She must have lost her phone ... that must be it, I think.

So, I need a strategy for this evening. Got it. Turn up on time, buy her a drink, kiss her on the cheek and leave. Quick dhansak and Punjabi Merlot down the Taj on my own and safely tucked up at ten.

I pour a glass of whisky to toast my resolve and my plan.

I shave, shower, and dress: casual shirt, chinos, loafers and anorak. OK, I'm lying about the anorak but I wanted to puncture the middle-aged preppy image I've probably just conjured up. I brush my somewhat flowing, sadly greying, locks back and think, not bad for a fifty-something old bloke. I could probably make a younger women very happy – only not the one I'm meeting tonight as we tried that for sixteen years and barely managed it once.

Scotch, fag, and I set off.

The shopping centre is closed at this time of the evening so I walk around the block and along the pedestrian precinct. There's the usual gaggle of ne'er-do-wells hanging around. There are a couple of shaven-headed, twenty-something nutcases swigging lager from their cans and swearing effusively and effectively at everyone who passes.

There's a gaggle of kids gathered around one of the benches drinking cider and alcopops. I've always sympathised with kids who have such a shit social life that they have to congregate on street corners, or pedestrian malls, or parks to have a decent drink. In my day it was illicit cans of Tennent's (with the pictures of the Tennent's lovely on the can providing a double delight of seventies erotica) at a youth club when such things existed. As long as the kids are not smashing anything up and being safe, I'm cool with them. I stop to light a cigarette (come on, give me a break, I'm nervous, right?) and I glance over at the group. The girls are dressed in the fashion of the day, which means they're barely dressed at all. A couple of kids are snogging. One of the boys catches my eye and defiantly says to his mates, so I can just about hear, 'Dirty old bastard.' The group turn to look in my direction, including a girl who has until now been wrapped around a seated boy, her back to me.

Our eyes meet.

Fucking hell it is my daughter Ailsa.

I stare. She stares back and in her look I feel her pleading. 'Please please please just go, don't say anything, don't embarrass me as you have all my life,' she is saying silently. The boy she's been snogging obviously feels there's an opportunity for a bit of fun. He's shaven-headed, with an earring and a tattoo – it just gets worse. He begins the phrase, 'You dirty old ...'

in a mock Steptoe voice – presumably passed down through the cultural ages from his father and his father before him – when Ailsa whispers at him, 'That's my dad,' or something similar and he stops mid-sentence.

I keep walking, but hold the lad's gaze. I am saying to him through my stare that if he hurts one hair on her head I shall rip him limb from limb.

Makes my blood boil. What are the police up to: spending all of their time catching speeding motorists, when they should be out stopping underage drinking and anti-social behaviour in the centres of towns and cities up and down the country? Think I'll write to the *Mail*.

Christ, I realise, I will have to get more involved in that girl's upbringing.

Well at least it's taken my mind off the next fifteen minutes, I think, as I head towards George's and the possible unpleasantness of telling Helen that I am leaving after just one drink.

I've always hated that place. In the nineties it offered a succession of increasingly bizarre fusion menus culminating in the gloriously, and not unsurprisingly short-lived, concept of the South East's only Welsh/Javanese restaurant. A couple of years back it hit gastro-pub status as a TV chef from Motherwell bought it. So, it started offering ponced-up pub grub: haddock and chips in Chardonnay batter, steak stuffed with black pudding with asparagus frites for forty quid a pop. And people with more money than sense flocked there mainly on the off-chance that said TV chef might actually do some cooking (and swearing) – rather than in Mayfair or Manhattan where his real business interests lay. It's now part of a chain of up-market French restaurants with obviously a Brit twist.

It's those little touches of faux working-class pretension that have always pissed me off in these places that by price exclude the working class. So the menu says 'fish and chips' or 'bangers and mash' or 'spotted dick' and you're meant to feel reassured that it's a regular place with normal pub grub – but when you look at the ingredients and the language used (everything's shaved or a terrine de ... or pan-fried – I mean for fuck's sakes what else would you fry something in ... a wheel barrow?) to say nothing of the prices that can only be described as legalised extortion.

But actually – worse than the menu, the prices and the impossibly lovely waitresses that are hand-picked for their aesthetic charm rather than waitressing skills – the real reason I hate this place is because of the clientele. Braying wealthy posing vapid stockbroking hedge-fund wanking bastards, all of them. Always.

Still. Live and let live, I always say.

I go in to be greeted by next year's new face of Dior. 'Have you booked?' she asks. 'I have no idea,' I say. 'I am meeting a friend for a drink,' I tell her, 'then I shall leave this fine establishment as quickly as possible, trust me on that.' She looks a little uncertain, but I am allowed to buy at the bar a large glass of house red for the price of a couple of reasonable bottles down the local offie.

I take a seat and wait. This is going to be easy. Peck on the cheek, finish my drink and out.

Ten minutes pass. I've finished the wine, so I order another one. I need the loo.

When I come back, Helen is sitting at the table with a bottle of Barolo.

'Your favourite,' she says, kissing me on the cheek. I sit opposite her.

Christ, she looks beautiful.

OK so the plan is scuppered immediately. One drink means finishing the bottle, certainly at the price she must have paid for that. So, finish the bottle, then you're out of here.

I look at her again. Oh fuck, she's perfect. Just the right amount of make-up, a white blouse open saucily enough to show cleavage and her eyes shine.

She looks fifteen years younger.

Talk to yourself now Jamie. Sort yourself out. You can do this. Together we – your conscience and what masquerades as your intellect – can beat the all-powerful serpentine sensation that is beginning to stir once again in your boxers.

'I have been trying to phone you all day,' I say tartly, I hope.

'I know,' she replies and smiles.

'Well why didn't you answer?' I say a little indignantly.

'Because, Jamie Gallagher, I knew you'd be trying to cancel this evening. And I didn't want you to.' She takes a drink of wine and looks me in the eye.

Goal flash. Cobra 1 – Rikki-Tikki-Tavi 0.

'I could just have stood you up,' I say, fighting, fighting, fighting.

'But you're too much of the gentleman to do that. Don't forget Jamie, I know you better than anyone else.'

I finish the house red in a gulp. 'I don't understand what the game is Helen,' I say.

'No game,' she says. 'It's just that you're turning back into the man I fell in love with all those years ago. Funny, sweet, charming. After a gap of sixteen years when you were a total pain in the arse. And I like you again.'

She fixes me with that look.

This is turning in to a romp for the cobra.

I take a slug of the Barolo and remember something important which temporarily breaks the spell.

'I saw Ailsa walking here. Practically fornicating in public with a yob outside M&S. Helen, what's happening with that girl? She's going completely off the rails. She just looked SO common'

'I know,' she said. 'She told me.'

'When?'

'I walked past her as well. Stopped for a chat with her and Nick. She said you'd glared at her. Oh, and that you were smoking again. That upset her.'

'Hang on a sec. Our daughter is behaving like a council-house trollop on a public thoroughfare with a bloke destined for Strangeways and I'm being criticised for having a smoke?' I ask indignantly

'Oh Jamie,' she says and strokes my hand. I'll stop the cobra analogy as it's turning into a first half rout. 'Nick's a good lad. He's got short hair because he's in the Officer Training Corps. He wants to go to Sandhurst after Oxford.'

'The tattoo?' I whimper pathetically.

'It's washable. A joke. He puts one on every weekend just for a laugh.'

'The cavorting?'

'What else are they supposed to do at their age? They can't get into pubs and clubs because everywhere needs ID. Would you rather they were left alone at his house or Edward's? At least she's unlikely to get pregnant sitting outside Marks.'

'Well I am not happy about it,' I say, defeated.

'Relax, darling,' she says.

I try to.

We chat, reminiscing about when we first met in London all of those years ago. About how nervous she had been when she first met me especially as I had a bit of a reputation.

'For what?' I ask.

'Contemporary ceramics, I believe,' she replies, deadpan and, in response to my puzzled look, smiles and I realise she's made a joke and I was too slow to get it. 'You idiot,' she says. 'All the girls in the office fancied you. Some of the boys, too.'

To quote Paddy McAloon, 'Darling, it's a life of surprises.' My ex making me laugh.

She prattles on. I finish the bottle and order another, my plan in tatters.

She talks about one particular night. It was shortly after we'd started sleeping together. We'd been out in a smart bar in Soho and we'd been drinking. She had been sitting opposite me and her foot had suddenly appeared under the table and hidden from view started gently stroking my groin.

I have never forgotten that as it was right up there in the pantheon of great erotic moments in Jamie Gallagher's life.

'Do you remember what I did?' she says.

'A little,' I say, and lo and bleeding behold, I feel her foot in my groin and the toes start to do their work. Because of the table cloth, the activity is hidden from view (I check these things) and she's looking at me deadpan straight in the eye.

'Do you remember now?' she says, the toes still doing their work and I am lost, utterly lost.

7. Here Comes the Sun

I've been awake since five. I am confused. Hung-over. Tired. Guilty. Oh, and confused.

She left at about two in the morning. She had to get back for Ailsa, she told me. 'What about Edward?' I asked and she replied 'Silly old bastard is away at a conference. I phoned him before I met you so there's not a problem.' She pulled on her clothes, kissed me and left.

Left me feeling confused, hung-over etc., I refer you to the list above.

We'd got back to the flat (ironically stopping outside M&S for a snog and a grope), we'd pulled each other's clothes off in the living room and made love. And when we'd done that, we did it all over again. And again.

It was quite remarkable. Dear Friend, I assume you not to have voyeuristic tendencies (which seemingly separates you from 99% of the population), so I shall not bore you with the details. You do not wish to hear of every gasp and probe and lick and thrust. Well if you do, you won't get that from me.

Suffice it to say that it was marvellous, wonderful and beautiful sex. It was hungry and dangerous and passionate and giving and caring and gentle and brutal and needy and loving. It was dirty, it was explosive it was probing – it was, in some states of the USA, probably pretty much illegal.

The French call an orgasm *la petite mort.* I never understood before, but last night in that bloody woman's arms I could have died complete. On several occasions.

This is serious. No, it really is. It's so serious I need someone to talk to about it. But who? I wonder if there's an organisation out there that caters for people infatuated with their ex-spouse? I could go to a shrink I guess, except for the obvious fact that they're all a bunch of fucking charlatans. No, I need a good mate to whom I can pour my heart out, someone who will listen, someone who knows me and cares for me and understands that underneath this cynical visage beats a truly human heart.

Sadly – because over the last few years I have pushed away anyone with the least bit of interest in getting close to me, on the grounds that they're obviously fuckwits (Gallagher's Universal Fuckwit Theory, if you choose to look it up on Wikipedia) – there are very few obvious choices. The blokes I know would shake their heads, make a lewd gesture and proclaim, 'Go for it my son!' whilst making that ghastly screwed-up pig face that males produce in pubs when talking of sexual congress.

There's only one person I can think of who's qualified to analyse what is going on here, who herself lives unconventionally and who seems utterly unaffected by sexual morality, and that is dear old Lizzie – who cheated on me and dumped me for Phil (you may recall his father owned half of Wiltshire?) some thirty years back at university and who subsequently I very nearly bonked in a hotel adjacent to the M6 four years ago, but didn't. It's a long story, Dear Friend, and most of it thankfully has been told in that last sentence. Subsequently we've met on a few occasions in London, and we've done some serious – near professional – flirting, but nothing has happened beyond that.

So, I could speak to Lizzie but that's a long-term option as she live in Cheshire and Cheshire takes planning. I need help now and so I have to self-diagnose and treat.

I get a piece of paper out.

Fact 1 – married life started off dull and went downhill from there. Everything. The sex, the conversations, we led separate lives for most of the time.

Fact 2 – Prior to marriage, we'd been pretty good together. I was happy with Helen until her father died. Selfish old bastard.

Fact3 – Prior to her father's death the sex had been great but not in the same league as last night.

Fact 4 – The children coming into our lives turned the relationship from passion and fun to routine and dull. Not their fault, they didn't ask to come in to the world, but I am simply stating a fact.

Ah, Sigmund, I feel we're getting somewhere now.

Fact 5 – I have been, and partly continue to be, the crappest adult ever. It just has never suited me – hence my road trip a few years back to revisit every sad fuck I'd ever laid eyes on, to find the answer to why I was incapable of anything approaching contentment.

Oh, this is good, I think. Very good. So good in fact that a second career in therapy beckons.

So, I say to myself – wishing I had a *chaise longue* on which to languish languidly and alluringly – to conclude. What screwed your relationship with Helen was that children dragged you screaming unwillingly into adulthood. She was the right woman for you, you were in love with her or at least deeply attracted to her, and only lost sight of that because you didn't want to grow up. And the sex is much better than it ever was simply because we're both better at sex than we were before. Like some test bowler, we've only found our line and distance and true cutting edge towards the end of our careers.

Reckon I've just saved myself £90 in fees.

Having identified the issues accurately, I believe, I go back to bed and worry myself stupid about what to do about it all.

I sleep fitfully for another couple of hours. Then awake as I realise that I have a date for this evening that I have to cancel. Where is that fucking groundhog? I can't see another woman when I've just spent the previous evening depositing the contents of my scrotum into my ex-wife. It's just not on. It's just not on; it's not how I behave. I am many things but, as I may have said before, I am not a cad.

I get up and shower, drink a bucket of tea. I get the phone book out then remember that I don't know Christine's surname so I can't find her bloody number. What to do? Phone Helen? No. I must avoid that woman at all costs, I really must. There be dragons.

I decide to purge myself by going once more to the gym thus killing two birds with one stone. Firstly, I'll sweat some of the alcohol away and hopefully revive myself in time to avoid the hovering hangover. Secondly, the chances are I'll bump into Christine there. She looks like she's a bit of a habitual user. You don't get a backside as pert as that unless you work at it..

So, I pass a fairly dull and uneventful hour there, first of all checking the pool before sitting on a exercise bike for the duration from where I can see the car park. If she turns up, I'll see her.

She doesn't show up. I leave at about half eleven, feeling perplexed.

My life, I conclude as I drive home, has a momentum all of its own. I seem powerless to cause any change in it whatsoever. Stuff just keeps happening to me for no reason other than for the amusement of the gods. I imagine the bastards up there having a bloody good laugh at my expense. Two days back, one of them obviously said to his mates (OK, so we're assuming polytheism, ?) 'I know, let's throw Jamie and his ex-missus together and make her absolutely gusset-stretchingly irresistible to the silly sod. That'll be a bit of a laugh until the next tsunami.' And another god probably said, wiping a heavenly tear of heavenly mirth from his (alright, or her) heavenly cheek, 'And let's get his ex-wife's pert friend to hit on him at the same time. That'll be a larf alright' (don't know why, but I'm imaging this latter god to be a bit of cockney geezer). And how they'd have chortled as last night's events unfolded.

So, I have to take control, simple as that. This is only my third day of so-called retirement and obviously I'm not cut out for a life of solitary leisure. I am not safe out alone. I need to do things.

I park at my apartment and go out for a coffee. Over a large cappuccino, I think.

What to do? A hobby? Oh, I know I could shag myself senseless with my ex-wife, that's a good one, and at the same time be attracted to her divorced friend. No, be serious. Golf? Well no. Too middle-aged to be done seriously and too fucking annoying to be done casually. I remember my last time out at St Andrews. The humiliation was extreme. And it's a known fact that everyone who is a member of any golf club south of Morpeth is a Pringle-sweater-wearing signed-up member of the British Fascist Party. So golf, no. Sailing? Fuck off. I will not wear a blazer and deck shoes for anyone. Flying lessons? Oh don't be ridiculous. Plane or helicopter, both absurd, on the grounds of carbon footprint, time and danger. And anyway I like to be flown. There are few things in life as joyous as four large gin and tonics at thirty thousand feet. If I had a joystick in my hand at the same time then I'd never manage to open the peanuts.

Gardening? That would mean moving or getting an allotment. Too much effort all round. Set up a business? Well there may be something in that, but what? Life in the large corporation has hardly honed my entrepreneurial skills.

But perhaps I could hook up with someone, invest some money, be on the board. So, that's a possibility.

Then there's voluntary work. Maybe as a committed socialist (well, not voting Tory round here virtually makes you one), I should look at putting something back. I could work with underprivileged kids or old people. I could fundraise for the local hospice.

Right, excellent. That's another plan. I will investigate. Perhaps this will lead into a new career as local activist.

Then finally, there's the travel issue. I have both money and time, so perhaps I should go around the world, visit the Great Wall. Kayak in the Rockies. Swim with the dolphins.

Trouble is, you don't want to do any of those types of things on your own. And also, I've been to most civilised countries over the years through work. And that only really leaves Wales, and I'm not that much of an intrepid explorer.

So travel as such doesn't appeal, but in my impecunious years I had always fancied a property in France. Nothing flash, somewhere rural where I could enjoy the local wine, the fresh air, perhaps the mountains and the sea.

But ... what a tie. And would I like to do that on my own? It'd be a long drive and chances are the local restaurant will be full of folk from Farnham and the likes. So no, a French place doesn't make the short list.

I finish my coffee, mentally stick two fingers up at the gods as I, Jamie Gallagher, have control once more. I head back to the flat determined to start to research both my plans but am interrupted by the front doorbell ringing. As I open the door I hear a voice. 'Jamie,' it says. 'It's Helen.'

'Come in,' I say. She also looks incredibly sexy. She stands in front of me and we look at each other.

The next thing I know is that we're making love on the sofa. Then we're in bed again.

As I drift off to sleep curled up tight with my ex-wife, I curse the gods for their cruel omniscience.

8. Lay Lady Lay

She leaves mid-afternoon and I drift back into a dreamless sleep.

It's very strange. It's not even as if we're communicating on a particularly high spiritual level. We're not really communicating at all except physically. We have sex, stop, have a nap, a kiss and a cuddle and before you know it we're having sex again.

Madness. In the old days, there's was never this level of need, passion or indeed expertise. It's like we've mastered something.

But it's wrong, I know it's wrong. I don't cheat (NB as perhaps previously mentioned I am not a cad) and I shouldn't be encouraging her to. Poor Edward.

Poor Edward? Poor Edward? Oh, that'll be the Edward that took her away from you in the first place, that cuckolded you, and caused partial premature dementia through grief to his dull little missus Daphne (although to be fair, Helen has virtually sworn that no act of congress took place between them before she told me she was leaving). But even so, he's not to be pitied one iota, not for his morality but simply because he's the most tedious, fucking wanker ever to work in reinsurance. Yup, that bad.

But it's still wrong and it has to stop (that'll be my brain talking). My genitals remind me that it's the most liberating exhilarating fun I've had since discovering the bra section of my mother's Littlewood's catalogue when I was an apprentice adolescent pervert.

Right I say, getting out of the bed that smells of her and sex. I need – despite the entire pantheon of gods and what they throw at me – to start implementing some alternative arrangements. I need to go to London, I need to meet some old colleagues, I need to start to function outside of this small town and the Lorelei that is my ex-wife (well, she's getting my rocks off). I can see the cliffs and frankly they scare me

I make a phone call and arrange to meet George for lunch tomorrow.

How had I not thought of George first time round when searching for wisdom about women? George, my trusted number two at the Intellect Corp. – the behemoth business that had emerged over the last few years as a result of us buying up every other competing operation. George is, as one would say, 'a good lad'. Ten years younger than me, thinks I'm marvellous and inspirational, his business mentor and he's no slouch himself. CEO, earning a fortune, never married, happy. There were apparently rumours when he first appeared that he may be gay – formed I suspect principally because he was well-groomed, never married and seemingly happy. Oh and at an office night out he had seemed to play air piano a little too vigorously in accompaniment to Dancing Queen by Abba. 'Obviously gay,' said the seers around the water cooler.

Anyway, given that Lizzie isn't readily available to bare my soul to because of geography, and I think I know what her advice would be anyway (along the lines of 'Fuck yourself silly, darling, if it makes you happy'), George will be the next best person. Plus, he's promised to take the afternoon off tomorrow so we can have a good old-fashioned boozy lunch. Which is what right now I need.

OK, shorter-term strategic thinking needed now. Christine. What to do? The only possible way of getting her number is through Helen, and I don't have the energy for further contact. And anyway, what sort of a message would it give off that a couple of hours after taking her to the edge of heaven and back (assuming she wasn't faking it ...) if I, the father of her children, admit to having been partially seduced by her former best friend?

Fucking hell. I just need a trouserless Brian Rix (a reference which, if you get it, dates you immediately) to step out of the wardrobe to complete the growing conviction that I am indeed living in a Whitehall farce.

Well, two choices. Go or stand her up. And I can't do the latter (listen – I have principles) so go I must. But I shall behave, I shall not fall for her female charms.

Christ, Jamie I ask of myself. Since when did you become such a consummate babe magnet? Eh? I mean, you were a good-looking chap, but it wasn't as if you represented Great Britain in the Shag Olympics 1974–1992. You were too nice. Too shy except when fuelled by drink or drugs at university. Or swooped on and seduced. A girl had to virtually jump on when you were in your teens before you'd make a move. There was always that dread fear of asking someone out and being refused. Or trying for a snog at a teenage party in the seventies in North East England, and being told to fuck off. Then all your friends finding out that you'd been told to fuck off. So, you didn't really try for fear of rejection and yet more *post facto* humiliation.

Which meant of course that the good-looking girls either went out with the complete shits who'd love 'em and leave them, and were so utterly marinated in their own self-confidence that a few rejections here or there never bothered them. Or (and this was the most galling) they'd go out with the smart but ugly (we're talking ears like the Champion's League Cup handles, teeth like Ken Dodd ... you get the awful injustice of the picture I paint) kids simply because these boys were so far down the social pecking order that they had nowhere else to fall to and so rejection meant nothing. If you ask you didn't get and some of those goons asked.

So, no, my bedpost did not crumble due to the structural stress of so many notches (dad would have killed me anyhow).

So, Jamie my friend. Do not thyself flatter. She – bored, divorced and lonely – wants a night out. A night out I shall give her, no impropriety or bodily fluids (I'm right out of them at the moment anyway as it happens) shall pass between us. I can be civilised.

I spend the afternoon cleaning the flat and attempting to eradicate the smell of sex. Now, there's a product waiting to be launched by Procter and Gamble.

I check my emails. One is from the garage reminding me that I have £65k's worth of sports car to pick up tomorrow.

One is from oldpals.net telling me I have a friend request.

Fuck fuck fuck fuckity fuck.

I have been down that route before. My odyssey to find the woman that got away. The women that got away. The friends that got away.

And do you know what I concluded after my road trip? It was that the people in my past who I have lost touch with, are no longer part of my life for a reason.

It's because they're old and disappointed and sad and jealous and longing for their youth again because they can't face the disappointment of getting old. But I have learnt one thing in middle age: it's that you get once chance pal, to shag, marry, love someone ... and then the scene moves on. I had accepted that, purged of the past, grown up, sorted, but then came home to find the Helen–Edward situation unfold in my own living room. So, I care not about oldpals.net, about trying to track down that girl at that Christmas party in 1982 that I kissed in the downstairs loo at a house party I probably gatecrashed.

What was her name? She was really nice. Good kisser, I recollect. Wonder what happened to her ...

See? See what access to the past does to you? It immediately takes your mind off the present. And the future. Which is a bad thing. Believe me, I know, I was that soldier: I found the significant others and found them to be, with a couple of exceptions, insignificant. And discontented and hurt and aging and disappointed. I've done all this above. You get the picture.

The past, someone wisely said, is another country.

A little like Luxembourg.

Only rather more disturbing.

So no way am I getting lured back in to that past nonsense. No way. I delete the email unread and vow to remove myself from the site.

Plan. Meet Christine. Talk to Christine. Do not, under any circumstances look at Christine's breasts, bottom, eyes, hair or ankles or pac-a-mac should she be wearing one. Just don't. Be civilized, try to enjoy her company, have a nice meal, don't drink to excess and at the end of the evening peck her on the cheek, see her to a taxi and leave. Sober and sated. Easy.

It's known as 'being adult' I believe, and I'm truly ready to try it out for the very first time.

9. Mother of Pearl

OK, so we are to meet at eight. I will get there at eight. I shave and shower at six as I am at a bit of a loose end. I'm standing in front of the mirror at 6.30 and I quite like what I see. Dark blue shirt, chinos, loafers and luxuriant (OK – if rather greying) hair brushed back. Not bad for fifty-two in a certain light if I say so myself once more.

Fuck, I've an hour and a quarter to kill before I can legitimately leave the flat. I fancy a wee drink.

No! I speak to myself in no uncertain terms. Be in control, you don't need alcohol. Make a cup of tea. I do just that and sit in front of the TV. It's the local news. Depressing. Parents of some kid – who has decapitated himself whilst driving a car at 2 am on an industrial estate killing himself (obviously, keep up, he's been decapitated) and his pregnant, underage girlfriend whilst off his face on lager and pills – blaming the police for giving pursuit.

A slightly past the sell-by date weather girl (who has become something of a local legend for allegedly servicing all the employees of the local fire station one after another, so rumour has it) tells me it might rain tomorrow but it might not.

Fuck. Ten to. I know. I'll find a documentary. I surf the TV channels and find a past episode of *Time Team* where they dig up a field in Gloucestershire hoping to prove it contains the headquarters of the Ninth Legion. Fifteen minutes later, two Samian pots, a couple of denarii from the Augustan period and lots of hairy archaeologists getting overly excited, and they've proved fuck all.

Bored. The news at seven. Global warming, house prices plummeting, shares in free fall, government ministers you wouldn't put in charge of a tombola at a church fete because they'd fuck it up, explaining that all the bad stuff in the economy isn't their fault and would be even worse if the fuck-witted opposition held power.. The country being run by utter incompetents.

I want a drink.

I look in the cupboards. Some rice wine. Nope. Some sherry. Why? Pernod? Come on? No I need some proper alcohol just to calm down.

I leg it to the offie. Bottle of malt (on offer – OK? Daft not to take advantage) and a bottle of Châteauneuf. Oh and a Petit Chablis. And twenty B&H – two of which I virtually swallow whole on the way back to the flat.

OK so not long before I need to leave. Be sensible, I say, taking a wine glass from the cupboard. Sensibly I replace it. It's too big, a balled goblet that could house several goldfish rather than a wine glass. I choose a much smaller one. That will control my drinking intake.

See? Self-restraint is easy.

I open the Châteauneuf, pour a glass, light a ciggy and have a sip. Then another. Fuck me the glass is empty. Better have another.

You can probably see where this is going. Bottle finished in the blink of an eye, the only benefit in my small glass theory is the extra calories burnt in undertaking double the pouring activity.

I feel fine. I clean my teeth change my chinos as I seem to have splashed red wine down my crotch and to the uninitiated it looks for all the world as if a scrotal cist has burst.

And so I leave, back through the pedestrian precinct, past the middle-aged pissed cracked-up ne'er-do-wells, past the gangs of idiot braying youths practising for their careers in the Stock Market: it's *déjà vu* all over again (OK deliberate tautology for vague comic effect, you pedant. I'll flag it earlier next time) – except my daughter is not wrapped around a nascent Andy McNab this time. Not in full view of M&S security cameras anyhow.

I enter George's. Same snooty pretty young waitress who looks at me with disappointment. She obviously remembers that I'd left last night without actually dining, that the lady had paid for my alcohol, and she's thinking that frankly I am too old for two seductive nights out in succession. 'I'll sit at the bar,' I say in an attempt to be assertive, but the withering smile she forces ensures I still feel unwelcome.

I don't even know if Christine made a booking. I guess, I think with rising panic, that that should be my job. God I am so out of touch with this dating lark. I order a glass of house red and then with a shudder think, 'Is that what I am doing here? Dating? Is that what she thinks? How do I know?' And the wine comes and I slurp it back and I feel seventeen again back on Teesside not really knowing if the girl I am going to meet expects me to kiss her, or ask her out, shag her or marry her.

It strikes me with horror that women – girls in those days – have always been a mystery to me. I have just never got them, never understood them. Look at me now. A gibbering wreck. I finish the glass, stand at the bar to order another when I hear her voice. 'Jamie,' she says and I turn around.

I am instantly, despite the twenty-four-hour pep talk, the vow to mental and physical chastity, enchanted.

She has a beautiful smile on her face. Dark brown hair in a light bob, just enough make-up to enhance the delicate frame of her face, slightly high cheek bones, which combined with almond-shaped eyes, give a Slavic beauty to her English rose prettiness. And she's dressed casually: an understated pearl necklace (stop it, no need for smuttiness), some matching drop earrings, a white silk blouse and jeans. Studied excellence and indeed elegance, I consider.

I kiss her on the cheek. She joins me in a bottle of Barolo.

Stirrings in the trouser department despite myself. I'm so so weak.

'I seem to remember last time we drank together,' she says 'you palmed the Chilean Merlot off on us.'

Good God she's right I think, and I remember that evening when she and her husband came to the house. Helen and I had, I recall, been arguing for about the last fifteen years continuously and that evening was the culmination. I was very pissed before the guests had arrived and I had resented the younger, more talented, wealthier bloke and his rather pretty wife, neither of whom I had ever met, being in my house. I hadn't been consulted, they were not my friends and so by Christ I brought such petulance to the table that evening that I should have been banned from playgroup for life.

And she obviously remembers it all.

'Oh God,' I say. 'Are my sins to return to haunt me?'

'As I said in the sauna. It was a very funny night. Refreshing to see someone just not give a damn about what others think.'

We chink glasses.

'Erm. I haven't booked a table,' I say. 'Did you?'

'No,' she said holding my gaze, a slight smile of bemusement on her face. 'I assumed you would.'

I summon the new face of Chanel to be told they are fully booked. No, they can't squeeze us in. Fuck off you middle-aged sex pest (I may have imagined that last bit).

I squirm in embarrassment. I'm not very good at this kind of thing, I tell myself in self-justification, then think, What? Not very good at booking a table in restaurant? I mean that's not exactly a high level of skill or talent needed there. It's not like piloting a hovercraft or making award-winning Wensleydale cheese, now is it?

'God I'm shit at this", I say aloud. She smiles

'That's nice to hear,' she says, smiling.

'We'll try somewhere else,' I say. 'How difficult can it be to get a meal on a Wednesday night in this town? There's meant to be a recession on.'

We decide to finish the wine then stroll round to the local up-market fish joint. It'll be the fat end of £200 I calculate, but for the first time in my life, glancing at Christine, I think it will be £200 well spent.

We chat. I deliberately drink slowly, not needing to get drunk (though to be fair I'm halfway there already). She tells me about Mike, how they'd met at University (Cambridge of course, and I decide it's better not to tell her about my Desmond from the only redbrick uni to have been turned back into a polytechnic). She'd been reading –reading, that's what they say at proper unis, reading, not studying – English. He'd been in the rugby team and rowed and she'd met him in her second year when he was doing finals. They fell in love, he went into the City, she trained as a teacher; within five years he was earning monstrous money and he'd insisted that she give up work.

'Why?' I ask.

'Dunno,' she said. 'I was a fool to agree. I loved teaching. But the circles he moved in, in London and then when we moved down here, the women stayed at home.'

'Like the 1950s,' I say.

'Exactly.'

'I would have loved Helen to have worked,' I reflected. 'Taken the pressure off me a little, but there was something in her psyche, upbringing whatever that means, that as soon as she got married, she stopped. I wasn't really consulted. She wanted to be looked after by her man.'

'To have babies?'

'Well yup, I guess so as she was four months pregnant when we married,' I say. I realise I don't actually know if Christine has kids or not.

I go on. 'I don't wish to come across all Germaine Greer-ish but I do feel let down. I mean when I was at uni the anti-sexist, ant-racist movements were so embedded in the music and culture and I really believed in it all. Dead right, women should have equality, have the right to work hard and juggle the family and kids with their partner. And yet look at it. All that education has gone to waste, in our generation, at least.'

Blimey it sounds as if I care.

Which actually, I do.

'Jamie,' she says drinking a glass of the red stuff. 'You're an enigma.'

'Is that good or bad?' I ask her.

'It's good,' she says. 'Very, very good.'

She holds my gaze. 'All bluster and not a little arrogance, but there's a kind compassionate soul in there somewhere.'

There is a danger here, I realise, that I might become enraptured. The trousers. They are stirring slightly. And truly I don't want them to. Get a grip, I tell myself, she's probably just being friendly. Lonely, you're someone safe to talk to.

We finish the bottle and leave.

Of course, you've guessed it. No room at the fish place. The other decent restaurants in this now seeming gastronomic hotspot of the South East are all spread out over the town in locations that to walk to them speculatively would be a waste of good drinking time.

So, in the High Street, to the backdrop of gales of laughter and satisfaction from the happy diners all around us, I phone the next best restaurant.

Full.

I try two more. Both full.

I look at Christine. 'I am such a dick,' I say. 'I am so sorry for ruining your evening.'

'Well Jamie, you know how to make a girl feel special,' she says, leaning towards me and kisses me on the cheek.

Enchanting. But also could be read as a simple sign of affection between friends.

We narrow it down to an upmarket burger joint, Pizza Express, the Chinese or the Taj.

I make her choose. I do know how to make a girl feel special after all, I tell her.

So we end up sipping lager and then toxic Côte du Rhône (you do expect more when you're spending £14.99 on a bottle ...) eating passable Indian food and the evening flashes by. She's bright (obviously), far brighter than me (yeah all right, you'd pick a ball of plankton for your pub quiz team before me ... yes, very funny), terribly well-read and very, very sweet. And very attractive.

I hear the gods absolutely pissing themselves right now as they see me sitting there baffled, bemused, mildly aroused, and not a little fascinated and quasi-tumescent.

She tells about Mike leaving. It had come a as surprise, she'd not thought of him as affair material and she'd suspected nothing. They had barely seen each other given his crazy hours and travelling, but when he'd come home that night to tell her the marriage was over she'd just felt numb.

'I actually pity him,' she tells me. 'He's a good man at heart, he's just been ... corrupted by the world he found himself in. The Big Swinging Dicks he worked with. Sounds like I'm making excuses for him, maybe I am, but I know he realises he's made a mistake.'

'Would you take him back?' I ask.

She hesitates before saying 'No. Never. I pity his stupidity and his selfishness and you can't love someone you pity, can you?' Again, she holds my gaze.

'Is he still with his PA?'

'Yup, silly cow. They have two kids together.' She pauses then goes on, 'Maybe I pity myself. We tried for kids but it never happened and he left before we found out why.'

This is moving a million miles away from the light-hearted flirt territory of earlier.

'I'm sorry,' I say and resist the urge to touch her hand in solace. She's already made her feeling clear on the subject of pity.

The first pause of the evening is broken when she asks 'What about you Jamie, are you over Helen yet?'

I'm pissed but not pissed enough yet quite to say that this morning I was over, under, sideways to and upside down with Helen. But that mental image did appear and I quickly suppressed it. I take a swig of wine, my mind in slight turmoil. What should I say? The truth? That we've been shagging each other senseless for the last forty-eight hours? So why am I out with Christine? Or rather, why am I still out with Christine and enjoying being so?

'Well, it's kind of complicated,' I begin tentatively. 'You see, the last few years had been terrible for both of us. That night you and Mike came round, that was kind of representative of the marriage on any night of the previous sixteen years. Rancid. The truth of the matter is we married too soon out of necessity. And a bit of carnality.'

'Must have been awful,' she said again holding my gaze. 'Only a bit of carnality?' Jeez she's flirting again (I think) and I don't know what to do. 'At least I thought Mike and I were happy ... with quite a bit of carnality. When he was there.'

The unbridled beast that is my groin bursts briefly into life at this, dammit. To deflect it I say,

'Well the best place we got to was mutual tolerance, I guess. I worked hard, drank too much, stayed out of the way. We grew apart. Plain and simple. And I became, as you witnessed, a bit of a pig'.

'But ...?' she enquires.

'But I have to be honest and say that as of the last few weeks we've been getting on much better.' Oh, if only she knew how much better I thought. 'Surprisingly so. I mean, we were always pretty civil with each other around the kids. But I think we've maybe ... grown fond of each other again.'

'Oh, that's nice,' she said and smiled. 'In fact I spoke to Helen yesterday after we'd bumped in to each other at the pool. Well, you'd bumped into me at the pool.' Another smile, 'She'd said as much. Perhaps you're destined to be together after all?'

'Oh, I don't think so. Helen has Edward and he'll always look after her. That's all she needs.'

'But Edward is such a boring, pompous prick,' she says with passion and I think: I could fall for this woman. If I'm not very careful,

Except something starts to tug at what passes for my rational mind and distracts me from my trouserly stirrings. She's been speaking to Helen on the phone about me? I had no idea they were still close. I don't think Helen had ever mentioned her after that one disastrous night.

And another thing. How did she recognise me in the pool? She'd seen me once, five or so years back, I'm slimmer now than I was then and pretty damn obviously I wasn't wearing swimming trunks when last we met. How did she know it was me?

Choice. Interrogate her. Get a confession that there's something Machiavellian going on here and spoil the evening. Or enjoy the evening, see where it goes and worry about all this tomorrow through the hangover.

With utterly uncharacteristic common sense, I choose the latter option. But she doesn't.

'You're thinking,' she says fixing my gaze again, 'How did I recognise you yesterday when I'd met you only once before? And why was I talking to Helen about you?'

'Well, maybe,' I say. 'But it's no big deal, really ...'

She goes on 'Well truth is when we spoke in the pool I had a feeling we'd met but couldn't place you. It was the accent. Northern amalgam. Unusual. But then in the sauna, with the ridiculous fart situation, I kind of just knew, part guessed, it was you. Because that night at your dinner party you were very, very memorable.'

'Memorable for being a boorish quasi-Northern drunk?'

She smiles.

'And I'd bumped into Helen a couple of weeks back. Pure chance. We'd not seen each other in years, had a quick catch-up and a coffee. She told me all about the two of you. And she rang me yesterday and I told her we'd met.'

She looks at me and smiles. 'Just a series of circumstances, Jamie, that's all.'

I'm pretty much reassured by this until another thought hits me.

Why didn't Helen mention it? Why hadn't she said she knew Christine and I had met?

Oh those malevolent gods are going to get such a bollocking should we ever meet. What is going on in my life?

I can't resist asking. 'Did you mention that we were meeting tonight?'

She hesitates and smiles, then says, 'Do you know what, Jamie? I think I may have forgotten to mention it ...'

We leave the restaurant. I suggest a nightcap but she says she has to go. Which I think is a good thing. The last exchange has caused me bafflement on an epic scale and I needed some space to digest it.

I walk her to the cab rank at the station. There's a taxi there waiting. She gives a fancy sounding farmhouse address in a village outside of town and as I am about to thank her for a lovely evening when her mouth is on mine. She tastes, despite the curry and the wine, fragrant and her tongue very swiftly passes over my own.

It's a very sensuous feeling.

Eventually she pulls away. 'Good night,' she says, puts a piece of paper in my hand and swiftly gets in to the cab. It pulls away. She waves out of the window.

I stare after her.

'Practically fornicating in the street, Dad?' says a voice from the shadows behind me. 'That's just *so* vulgar.'

I turn around to find Ailsa smirking at me. Beside her are some eight of her friends. Smirking at me also.

Fuck tit bollocks cock arse: not necessarily in that order. I think that just about sums my particular predicament up rather well.

10. Party Party

I awake at four. Thank God I am not lying beside the Fragrant Christine this morning, or indeed my nearly-as-fragrant ex-wife, as my guts are back to Krakatoan standards. Actually, Krakatoa the exact instance just before she blew.

I leg it to the toilet.

Christ that curry was hotter than I remember. No Christine, or indeed any woman, would not have appreciated Jamie in all his four o'clock splendour.

I drift back to light sleep that is seeded with demonic dreams. I am in a coal scuttle. The lid is lifted by Ailsa. Edward and I are clamped in embrace together.

Christine says hello to me as I stroll down the street dressed as Dr Miriam Stoppard.

There was one too involving Captain Birdseye and a large haddock that I shall not give more detail about as I think I need professional help unpicking that.

I sit and ponder the previous evening when I wake from these eerie slumbers. My mind drifts over an image of the simple beauty and undoubted intelligence, of Christine. And that kiss. The gentle intimacy, the confidence that I would not reject her.

Even in my current bemused state, my trousers, indeed my PJs, stir.

Then there was what Ailsa saw: and yes, that does make me want to roll up and die. That's excruciatingly embarrassing for all parties and I do feel somehow as if I've been caught doing something wrong, but why? I'm not married to her mother any more – Helen walked out on me. OK, granted there was the vague hypocrisy of a very public display of intimacy in the light of my rant about her M&S antics, but why do I feel as if I've been caught in bed with the vicar's wife, by the vicar himself? Why do I fear the consequences of Ailsa telling Helen what she saw?

Eventually two more curried visits to the lavatory later – God I am glad I live alone – it reaches 7 am and the start of the new day proper.

Time to pick up the car, go for a spin and then head up to London to meet George. I need a chat, male company and a wise man's counsel over a boozy lunch – that'll sort me out and take me away from the temptations of this fucking place.

Shower, shave, breakfast; if it weren't for the immediate post-espresso need to visit the toilet again (I wonder briefly if there is a category for this in the *Guinness Book of Records*) I'd be feeling quite good. But then that niggle – what's going on, if anything, between Christine and Helen?

Why would Christine be interested in me? I don't want to do myself down overly. I'm not a bad looking fellow for my age, as I believe I may have mentioned. Where once I was dishy, perhaps I'm more side-dishy now. Petri-dishy, perhaps. But Christine is four or five years younger than me and looks ten years my junior. She could get anyone she wanted. Why me, when her only real point of reference for me is as a drunken boor?

Motive? I can see several. She's attracted to drunken boors. She's attracted to artists formerly known as drunken boors. She's got something against Helen and wants to get one over on her or ... roll of the drums ... she knows I'm loaded and that's what attracts her.

Fuck it, I think. Here we go again, overthinking, over analysing a situation that a lot of blokes would kill to be in. Shut the fuck up and enjoy the day, I tell myself unconvincingly.

Smart casual dress and at half eight I leave the flat and walk the twenty or so minutes across town to the Mercedes garage.

I walk passed the stacked-up traffic containing stressed men and women on their way to dull jobs and I think that I am a lucky man. OK, I'm not quite sure what the hell is happening in my life and perhaps two lovely women and the gods are conspiring against me to cause some as yet unseen humiliation, but at least it's not dull.

Go with it I continue to tell myself. It's what you've longed to be for all those years of marriage and parenthood and respectability. You wanted to be different. Interesting. Unconventional. Windswept, mysterious and poetic. Heathcliff of the Home Counties (obviously without the premature deaths and psychopathic tendencies. Oh, OK and pain in the arse gruff Yorkshire ways. But please can you stop being so fucking literal when I'm soliloquising ...?)

I have to leave the town for a few days and sort my head out.

But first let's get this little beauty that is my car.

I walk into the showroom. The receptionist looks at me initially with barely disguised disgust then manages, nearly in time, to hang a sickly welcoming smile on her face. 'Peter will be with you in a moment, sir,' she says. Then 'Coffee?' I accept.

That'll be the most expensive cup of coffee I ever have.

I sit down and wait for Peter. I pick up the *Daily Mail* and learn from the headline and first two paragraphs that ISIS are destabilising the housing market by putting the anthrax spores in the water supply.

Fuck that's pretty worrying I think. Thank God they've told me. I can prepare properly now. Then Peter arrives all beaming smiles and pumping handshake and momentarily I forget about this image of global doom and negative equity. I am just so shallow. We sit at his desk and he goes through the various bits of documentation, registration forms and service schedules and the like.

He takes me to a glass space where under a silk cover my car (presumably) sits. With a flourish, he pulls the cover off and I try to look suitably impressed at the limp theatre my money has bought.

We sit in the car. It has that unique new car smell, which is just as well as if there'd been a whiff of nun's gusset it would have gone straight back.

He talks me through the controls, the sports gear button and the booster and force shields to repel Klingon death rays – and I'm not really listening. I'm a little bothered, I have to say, about the bucket sports seats which appear to be forcing my own backside into some kind of restrictive mould. Think of a dwarf attempting to sit in a shire horse's shoe (Oh for fucks sake, I don't know why a dwarf would want to do that – go with it for God's sake). Perhaps I should have test driven it. I'm a little scrunched – these Germans have been economic with the legroom.

And my head brushes the ceiling.

I have a bit of a fiddle with the seating and find a driving position that does not qualify me for Contortionist of the Year.

The seat heats up. 'That's the heated seating, sir,' Peter explains pedagogically, and I say, 'It's nearly seventy degrees in the middle of summer. How do I turn it off?' He shows me.

Last thing he does is hit a button and the roof folds up into itself with a soft purr.

We get out of the car. He goes to the boot, takes out a massive bouquet of flowers (about as much as the boot can hold I subsequently learn), and shakes hands again.

First time I've been bought flowers. I'm rather touched.

The glass door of the room opens silently and off I jolly well go.

Well strictly speaking off I jolly well try to go but I career forward stopping inches from hitting the stationary car on the forecourt in front. Fuck I think. I take six attempts to get the little fucker in reverse and eventually manage to swing into the stationary traffic. That's better I think.

I was wrong.

I just cannot get the hang of the fucking automatic gear box. I've not driven an automatic car for years. Every time the traffic moves forward, I over-rev and the car lurches forward narrowly missing the poor bastard in front.

A couple of lads walk past on their way to work in one of the industrial units. After a particularly spectacular lurch forward, they point and smile at me. One of them shouts to me 'Ask Santa for some driving lessons next Christmas, mate!' and they both laugh.

I hit what I assume to be the on switch for the radio, and boiling hot air spews out chest high. I really should have listened to Peter. I am beginning to realise. Eventually I find the right button. I swear the space shuttle would be less complicated to manoeuvre around the industrial estate than this fucking car. The radio bursts in to life. The Bee Gees wail about 'Night Fever'. It's very loud, the traffic begins to clear ahead, and I have to try to press the accelerator steadily enough to go at thirty miles an hour and I dare not take my eyes off the car in front because I know I am within a minor lapse of concentration from hitting it.

'Night Fever' melds into 'Staying Alive'. Oh joy – here I am in the rush hour, driving through town with the roof off my car, blaring possibly the shitest pop music ever produced at a volume that would have an Ibiza club owner reaching for his earplugs – and I can do piss all about it.

A bloke goes past on his bike and laughing, waves at me.

At the next set of lights I manage to kill the Bee Gees – sadly not literally – and with some dignity drive into town. I consider taking the car for a proper spin along the country lanes, but my nerves are frazzled and I fear something awful would happen if I did – like an hour long Chris de Burgh tribute on the radio, and me with no means of blotting the bastard out.

I manoeuvre into a parking space below my flat, eventually find the button that puts the roof back up, and try to sink into the driving seat in a relaxed relieved manner. Though the fucking seat ensures my internal organs are all squashed together like some rustic French terrine when I try to do this, so I get out to relieve the pain.

One of my neighbours sees me locking up and smiles.

Only yours truly could part with a wodge of cash on a new car and end up the centre of cruel mockery for the whole town. Perhaps this car was a mistake, I muse.

Anyway, I shall worry about that another day. I potter in the flat, watch some news then prepare myself for a lunch of excess with my old mate and sidekick George. George will sort me out; he'll talk sense as possibly the most immature and puerile (OK, a tautology but who cares?) bloke on the planet – no, I'll refine that – bloke in the Home Counties with the obvious exception of your good friend and narrator. George who's old enough to know better, who always turns up at company functions with women of exquisite beauty and sauciness. Occasionally one will get a double outing, but usually they're dumped quickly and he's on to – literally – the next quick as a flash.

George who can drink for twenty-four hours, smoke himself stupid and still function like a master in the boardroom.

George will indubitably sort me out. He has wisdom – certainly when it comes to women.

And so, reassured that I am on track for some kind of redemption, I head for the station. I buy a *Guardian* – old habits die hard. I actually find their anachronistic liberalism, mixed with articles such as 'The Top Ten Avocado Face Washes for Men' irritating in the extreme, but as an anachronistic liberal myself I cannot migrate to another broadsheet.

As the train pulls off, I think back to the years of commuting I put up with. Of rickety 1960s slam-door rolling stock that was hot in summer and freezing in winter. Of smoking compartments. Then when I started to do well, I left my working-class roots (irony-right?) and began to travel first class. Resolutely never talking to anyone despite the fact that at times I spent more time with my travelling companions – especially when there were leaves on the line – than I did with my own family. Surrounded by captains of industry and traders and bankers all heading off to the City to wreak havoc on the financial markets of the world, I felt strangely superior.

God knows why frankly. Superficially I was the same as them for so many years regardless of industry or (alleged) expertise. But no, I wasn't the same, not in my heart. I didn't listen to the same music or read the same books or take the same newspaper or –and here was a very large difference – vote the same way. They were all rabid Tories whilst I through the Foot/Kinnock wilderness years, had held the candle for true socialism and despised the right-wing junta that was running the country.

Of course, I see now this was all bollocks. I was just the same as them in deed, and that was more important than thought or inclination. I was one and the same without realising it. Socialist? Me? Sure thing, I respected the integrity of the working man and his right to lead a dignified and rewarding life as long as it was far away from me so that I didn't need to listen to his dim opinions, hear his whinging brat children and their estuary vowels. I'm all for the working man as long as I don't have to share a lift with him. And of course, a worker must have the right to withdraw his labour, but I used to hate the bastards when that meant a train strike stopped me getting into work. I was a Hugo Boss Bolshevik, a Chablis Commie, and a Château Margaux Marxist.

OK I'm being a little hard on myself but, in the main honest, I think as the train charges through the Home Counties towards the 'Smoke'. I realise, with a blinding flash of self-enlightenment, my problem once more. It's what caused the break-up of my marriage; it's what made me drink excessively throughout my adult life; and it what is making my relationships with Christine a non-starter; and causes me to continue to hump Helen at the drop of a hat (or her underwear).

I've never grown up. And I have to keep reminding myself of this.

Hence the hanging on proudly to the music I liked in my youth. The secret smirking at crass childish humour, the inability to take on board, body and soul, the mantle of 'adult'.

Take this journey. Until a few years ago a piece of graffiti on a wall between London Bridge and Waterloo East used to amuse and fascinate me every time I saw it, which was most days. It's been painted over now but for many years there it was, on the left-hand side in a builder's yard if you were heading towards Waterloo. High on the wall were writ, large for all the world to see, the words 'Big Daves (sic) Gusset'. It's obsessed me from when it first appeared. Who was big Dave? And why the interest in his gusset? Was it its size, its consistency, its odour, that made it so noteworthy? Or is it post-ironic and that an underwear-less Dave did not indeed have a gusset?

So for all those years each and every day I'd have a wry smile certain, absolutely certain, that I was the only one on that damn train of misery who noticed this thing. Everyone else was busy talking loudly in to their phones or reading the *FT* determined on the battlefield of business and high finance to shine, to beat their competitors, to win through sheer hard work alone. And then there was me, self-absorbed deliberately in what I saw as irreverent free-spirited humour.

And that, I used to think, was to be admired and made me stand out. Yes, I took my job seriously – in as much as I had a house and kids to support – but I thought differently to the careerists around me. They got on through hard work, application mixed with a massive dose of arse-licking; I got on through innate genius and the ability to think utterly differently from the norm.#

In truth, I see it now. I was just wanting to be different, eclectic, irreverent – when actually I was just being a dickhead. So determined was I that I wasn't going to conform to the norms of adulthood, I deliberately thought – and occasionally behaved – as if still stuck in the body of an adolescent. I reckoned it to be endearing, the irreverent puerile humour – and maybe to some of my colleagues (if not my wife and her friends) perhaps it was. Or maybe I was just overly indulged by the people who worked with and for me.

Helen always used to tell me to grow up. I took it as just part of her general contempt for me, but I have begun to understand something very specific in this journey and as we head over the river to Charing Cross.

I am emotionally stuck somewhere in the early 1970s. I have to grow up. Or start wearing tank tops again.

Perhaps it's actually a condition that can be treated?

11. Sympathy for the Devil

I'm trying to explain my new theory to George but he's not having any of it – partly due to the fact that I suspect he's suffering from the same condition as me, but mainly due to the fact it is now five o'clock in the afternoon, we're standing outside a pub in Covent Garden having a smoke and we've been drinking since midday.

Needless to say, he was having none of the grown-up argument and suggesting a late-night shopping trip to some retro store he knew in Soho that actually specialised in tank tops. His theory was that all blokes longed to be subversively adolescent but only a few – he and I really – had the nerve to act on it. 'No really, mate,' he was pontificating 'the norm should be for blokes to laugh at farts and knob gags. Everyone does it, even if just mentally. They think it. Trust me. Bet the Pope himself ogles the nuns from his Vatican window and chuckles when a cardinal lets one rip accidentally.'

We discuss the Pope and nuns, well more nuns really, at length, finish our cigarettes and go back into the bar for another drink.

It's the usual early evening officer worker crowds interspersed with a few builders and scaffolders who've snuck in without having to take the entrance test to prove they're middle class (this is a trendy Covent Garden establishment, you know). I've yet to tell him of my women problems. God knows what we have actually been talking about , considering we've been in each other's company for a large part of the day.

A couple of drinks, a catch-up, a meal, more drinks, footy, work reminiscences do-you - remember when we pushed the piano into a lift at a sales conference in Jersey? Do-you-remember that MD being caught in bed with the south-east representative when the fire alarm was accidentally set off in the middle of the night. And was it accidental? The usual happy chatter that blokes with too much time on their hands talk about when alcohol is taken. And so here we are pleasantly slaughtered and about to buy yet more alcohol and talk yet more shit.

And do you know what? I feel embarrassed for him and for me. He's a noisy drunk and there's nothing worse for other people just trying to have a quiet pint than to have to overhear middle-aged guys catching up. I'm aware we should know better. I'm aware too that I'm feeling uneasy. This isn't me. I'm not a bar-room boor and yet here, this afternoon, I'm doing a fabulous impression, word-perfect, of being just that.

But still – when I've managed to nab a booth at the back of the pub where we're not quite so close to other people and less likely to get thumped for irritating the other drinkers – I decide it's time to tell him of my predicaments. He listens. He looks at me in a queer way, as they would have said in the forties, takes a swig of ale and says as if it's as plain as the rather reddening nose on my face 'Shag them both. And their mothers and their aunties. Listen mate if you're still a babe magnet at fifty seven,' I ignore the very deliberate ageist inaccuracy, 'looking like that,' he looks me up and down in something approaching disgust 'then good on you and go for it.'

I suppose I expected little else. In fact I think, in truth I've only introduced it into the conversation because I'm (Jesus I hate to admit this) a little proud. Me. Middle-aged me. With women seemingly throwing themselves at me. I take another swig. So what if my daughter saw me snogging on the street? She should be proud that her old man's still got it. And no I don't feel guilty. Helen walked out on me, remember? I didn't start this, right.

Well OK, wrong, I realise drunkenly with a flash of temporary sobriety: maybe I did get ripped a few too many times, maybe I did constantly look to bite the middle-class hand that fed middle-class me. I could have acted differently, I could have changed ... but I force down this wave of self-analysis knowing this way lies dragons, if not madness, if not mad dragons.

So I am enjoying the adulation, albeit rather reluctantly, displayed by George. He keeps going with a few more grains of wisdom and we have another drink. Then a smoke. Then we adjourn to a local hotel he knows where we consume a bottle of Chablis. We do it very quickly as the doorman, who looks like an ex-paratrooper, has come over and told us that other guests are being disturbed and that he'd like us to leave. George doesn't immediately agree and becomes not a little belligerent. I try to calm him down realising that George, unlike myself, does have a tendency to being a nasty drunk. 'You'll have to make us leave, pal,' he says to the doorman who looks like he could easily eject both of us with one hand tied behind his back.

'C'mon George,' I say, apologising to the doorman and slipping him twenty quid, 'we're leaving. Sorry.'

As we do, I see our reflections in the mirror and it's not a nice image. We're two drunk, noisy middle-aged blokes who should know better. And I feel a little ashamed.

On the pavement I say to George, 'Right I'm off home, I'm getting a cab to the station.'

George is having none of it. 'Nope,' he says defiantly, 'we're going to a little club I know. You'll love it mate.'

'What kind of club? Jazz ...?'

'Yeah, something like that,' he says and I think, a bit of mellow music at this time of night might well work wonders.

'One last drink – a nightcap George, just one alright? Just to please you.'

We hop a cab that slices through the heart of Soho and I think oh shit no, not one of those awful tourist strip joints where they charge you three hundred quid for a bottle of Cava, and Russian crims or Welsh thugs depending on the racial mix of the bouncers march you to the local cash point and attempt to empty your bank account on the promise that you will remain loosely connected to your testicles if you agree to their demands. Surely not George? I don't want to see some poor girl off her face on drugs bump and grind on stage to a shit Tina Turner record, in an attempt to arouse the libido of the sad fuck blokes watching her.

Just as I start to tell him this, we're crossing Oxford Street heading away from the sexpots of Soho town, cutting across Regent Street, and heading north through Marylebone. 'You'll love this place, mate. Absolutely love it. Remember Cindy at the last Christmas party? I met her here.'

Oh Cindy incidentally, I recall. Do I remember her? To have forgotten her would have been sacrilege: like meeting the Virgin Mary, having tea with her, interviewing her and her host of angel mates, then forgetting to tell anyone about it. A Christmas party two years ago at some swanky bar in Mayfair. Some people's partners showed – bored, nervous folk thrown into the netherworld of an office they had only experienced second hand; most there only to keep their partners from groping Henry or Henrietta from accounts or because they were the designated drivers to get them home to the suburbs safely.

George had arrived with Cindy and the party collectively held its breath. She was super- model gorgeous, dressed in a little black number that showed enough chest and thigh to have every single man there trying to have a peek and every single woman green with envy hating her. She'd smiled, she'd danced, she'd hung on every word George said and to everyone there they looked like a couple in love. I have to say at the time I was a little puzzled why such a great-looking girl was spending her time with my mate George who must have been fifteen years her senior, but I pushed the thought from my mind. That was me slipping in to my old nasty cynical ways. He'd found true love. Good luck to him, the jammy bastard.

When she wasn't mentioned again after the party season had died down, I thought little of it except that he liked to keep his private life to himself. When I did ask a few months after he'd looked a little puzzled. 'Cindy ...? Oh Cindy from the party? Nah that was never anything serious.'

So I hadn't put Cindy down as a jazz aficionado when I'd met her.

We pull up somewhere in Maida Vale, not a part of town I know. There is a Victorian house with a grilled front door where two shaven-headed thugs – who looked like Serbian war criminals – stand outside, dressed in full black tie gear with earpieces and microphones. Georgie bounds towards them and they stand still and tall, looking at him imperiously, arms folded with a 'You shall not pass unless the Komandant says so' look – which disappears when George flashes a gold card at them. I am ushered in, sign the guest book then we walk up an unpromising flight of stairs to a massive oak door.

George opens it and we walk in.

There are dimmed lights everywhere and soft jazzy music so George has not been lying about the genre of music at least. For a moment my eyes take time to adjust to the lighting. When they do I see a bar, much smoke (the smoking ban is obviously being ignored I think, somewhat self-righteously).

And girls. Oh Reader, what girls. Over twenty of them, all at a glance beautiful and young. Dark-haired, blond ... slender, fulsome ... tall, less tall.

Beautiful girls.

I haven't really had the time to take it all in before one of them, tall, dark shining hair as if she has stepped out of a shampoo advertisement, takes my hand and says in a seductive East European accent, 'Buy me drink'.

Now call me dense but after the day's intake of alcohol I have experienced, I am only just beginning to realise that this is no ordinary social club. Perhaps the fat, middle-aged business men scattered around the room being fawned on by these beautiful young woman should have given the game away a little sooner.

My only other experience of a similar place – fifteen years ago in a 'nightclub' in Sofia – had ended up in my being mugged and robbed when I'd left before it was deemed polite to do so. I didn't want to make the same mistake here I reason, and besides my newly found companion, who told me her name was Irena, is rather charming.

I feel obliged to buy her a drink, resistance being useless, so I go for the cheapest bottle of white wine at £100.

Fucking hell I think. Just been mugged again.

We chat. She is a language student from Poland. She came here, she told me, to earn money for her sick mother and father. Oh, I sympathise and said that she is a good daughter.

'I good fucker too,' she says. 'Five hundred quids I fuck you good.'

Oh Irena, I think drunkenly, looking in to her dark eyes, feeling her hand reaching to stroke my cock under the table. Oh, Irena is there no innocence, no purity left anywhere in the world? Plus if you're a language student you need to work on some basic grammar, young lady. I consider deconstructing that last sentence for her and showing her the error of her ways, but I suspect that right now she's probably not in student mode.

I pull her hand away and tell her politely 'No thank you. Give me the details of your sick mother and I shall send her money myself.'

She looks at me as if I were mad. 'You madman? You prefer boys? I get boys,' she says a little too enthusiastically.

I know there was little point in trying to explain. About innocence. About purity.

George on the other hand seems to be enjoying having his epiglottis stimulated by a busty blond, and suddenly I feel a sadness for the world. The song playing is inappropriately 'Funny Valentine', the Chet Baker version I note for some reason. I go up to George and whisper in his ear, 'I'm off'. He removes the blonde's tongue with difficulty from his mouth and says with a smile, 'Already? Where you taking her?'

'Nowhere, George, nowhere,' I say. 'I'm just off, on my own. Away from this place. Truly we don't know each other, as I would rather die than be in a place like this. Sorry, mate,' and with that I head down the stairs caring not one jot if I am beaten to a pulp by the Serbian war crims. It would be preferable to spending even one extra minute in this hell-hole.

A taxi to the station, a late train home, a glass of shit fruit juice masquerading as wine and I feel as sad as I had felt in many a long time. Through the alcohol I feel ... lonely.

12. Mean Mr Mustard

I awake and the hangover and self-loathing kick in immediately, big time, once more. And these feelings, they're serious, they're not messing around or gently flirting with my well-being. The bastards, both physically and mentally, have joined forces as one insurmountable army and are out to flail me from the insides and rip out my soul.

I get some water, ablute unpleasantly and crawl back to bed. I long for sleep, but all I can see is that room full of high-class prostitutes and whilst ninety per cent of my sentient being is appalled and horrified, there's ten per cent that's still niggling away at me – despite the heartfelt moral indignation – intrigued and excited. Those girls were beautiful ...

I stop the ten per cent of my corrupt being from going there. What was I thinking being in such a place? How could I have been so naive? How could I have been so utterly knob-numbingly dumb? How could I have misjudged George all these years? I had him down as a successful babe magnet, whilst all along he was nothing but a vulgar little prostitute punter. OK, he wasn't kerb-crawling in Kings Cross, but actually what he was doing was even more exploitative. Creep. Saddo.

And yet Irena was very, very attractive.

And that thought in itself horrifies me in that – no matter how sexually enlightened I am, or at least try to be – I find myself appalled at the truth of this encounter which was that ... I found her very attractive, very attractive indeed. And part of me would – I am further appalled at this confession, too – part of me would have liked to ... further the encounter in some way.

Fuck me, I conclude, I am as bad in some ways as George and those ghastly fat, rich blokes in that place who allow beautiful women like Irena to be part of the people-smuggling sex trade that brings shame on men everywhere. That I can get excited looking down the dress of a smuggled sex worker (well, I'm guessing she was smuggled) makes me no more enlightened than I was when I was an adolescent growing up in 1970s England. Something wrong with you boy I think, always has been.

Those times in your teens when the site of a cleavage or thigh could engorge you for weeks ... I still recall the receptionist at the doctors' surgery, when I about fourteen, who wore incredibly tight sweaters and the effect she had on me. I'd gone in to see about a chest infection at my mother's insistence and walked out (barely) with priapism. No visit to a medical practitioners since has ever been quite so confusing.

Women were meant to be looked at – that was the culture of the times, bikini-clad girls on cans of Tennent's lager and in the pages of my parents' *Sunday Express* (a fairly vile paper in those days but nothing compared to mendacity dripping little-Englander fascist shit sheet it is now.)

Women were objectified sexually and we were brought up to some extent to do the objectifying. But men should by now have realised that that's wrong, and amended their behaviour accordingly. It's patently obvious we haven't. Well, maybe I haven't. Cut me and I am at heart nothing but a sexist product of 1970s North East of England.

I'm beginning to bore myself with this soliloquy of self-loathing. Christ the mood I'm in this morning, I could out-soliloquise Hamlet. I toss and turn and for about an hour continue to chew over the rancid cud of my day out and a friendship ended. And eventually I drift back into a light and unsatisfactory dream. I'm at the Merc garage and George is pulling me by the arm into the slave market that is at the back of the showroom (where the Service Desk should be, if you want a precise location) and there are hundreds of women standing partially naked, including Christine, Helen, my Aunty Moira, Valerie Singleton, Olive from *On the*

Buses and Irena (perversely fully clothed in a full-length anorak), and it's Valerie Singleton that I am about to choose ... I awake suddenly, sweating, worried, and only relieved that I had not chosen my Aunty Moira .

What am I to do? I feel battered, confused and massively perverted (at least in my subconscious) not least because of my obvious subliminal lust for *Blue Peter*'s finest. What next? Shep the dog for God's sake?

I need, I conclude, to relax, hide away somehow today. It's the weekend and all I have planned is a Sunday lunch tomorrow with my daughter. If, of course, she's still speaking to me.

I have a moment of rare relationship-building inspiration. I text her suggesting that she brings the shaven-headed, militaristic (but still thug-looking to my mind) boyfriend along. That should get me some brownie points somewhere.

So, what to do today? I need to escape, I need to think. I need to breath, away from all these torments that this – for fuck's sakes, my first week of alleged freedom – has brought me. Where to go? What to do?

I get out of bed, make a Vesuvian (see, I'm not just a one volcano sort of a guy) strength coffee and pick up the phone. It's blinking that there are messages. I ignore them, choosing to watch the news on TV instead.

Oh, I am so glad I've done that. War, pestilence, earthquakes, floods, drought, forest fires. Probably just missing locusts, boils and frogs from this particularly apocalyptic bulletin.

Oh, plus one of the world's oldest investment banks has imploded. Pictures from Wall Street of slick young men walking away from their work with all their possessions in cardboard boxes. Apparently the subprime mortgage market is shot to buggery. There's a surprise I think, sagely, never having heard the term in my life before.

There's some commentary about how it may impact the UK. I doubt that instinctively. Our banks might have been full to the gunnels with pointless, chinless wankers but they surely could not have been utterly clueless in what they've been doing? I mean, banks can't go bust, surely?

I'm bored with the gloom and surf the satellite channels. I stumble across Frasier and veg for an hour, wondering how the Americans – who are usually so humourless on the big screen and very often in real life – can produce such masterful small screen comedies.

Then I listen to my answerphone messages. One from Helen. Interesting: wants to know if I'm around at nine in the evening (that was yesterday). Said she'd try my mobile. My cup of torment positively runneth over.

One from Henry, my so-called accountant and financial advisor. He wants to meet as soon as convenient.

Well, he can fucking well wait. Probably just wants me to buy him lunch again.

I check my mobile and sure enough three missed calls from Helen and two from Henry. The two texts from Helen essentially asking why I'm fucking ignoring her.

There's part of me that's a little disappointed that Christine has not been in touch, but then I realise she doesn't have my number. I recall she passed me a piece of paper as she had got into the cab. I get up and find it stuffed in my jacket pocket.

I sit and look at it for some time, wondering what to do. After a couple of minutes, I add it to my contacts on my mobile.

Then I form an inspirational plan to sort my head out. It involves catching a train to Manchester and having lunch with Lizzie.

Lizzie, you may remember, is a remnant of my midlife crisis of six years ago. We were lovers at university, a long time ago. She was very posh and incredibly saucy in bed and I was awestruck by both these attributes, until I caught her being posh and naughty with Phil the thick rugger bugger who's Daddy owned half of Wiltshire ... OK, I'm aware I've told you all this several times before, and my repetition does not point to any obsession about this matter – how dare you say otherwise, frankly. Truly, I'm over this part of my past ...

Well to be strictly accurate I *had* got over that until my round Britain road trip of a few years back, when I tracked her down and we got pissed and we so very nearly slept together, but we didn't for a variety of reasons too dull to deal with here but mainly due to poor locksmithing.

Anyhow, we'd become good email mates of late and I'd see her when she was in London and we'd flirt and she'd suggest sex and I'd decline and I think secretly she was happy I did, as she thought it might become serious. Her husband was loaded and boring and she had a fairly active sex life in Manchester with a number of casual acquaintances.

Saturday I think is a good day for her. She'd told me her husband's law firm sponsored one of the local rugby league teams and consequently she'd moaned many times in the past about him spending more time with other chairmen than with her. 'I wouldn't mind dahling if it were rugger proper,' she'd explained once, 'but it's that flat cap L.S. Lowry version of a the game that these silly Northern men play that gets me down. I mean, where even is St Helen's for God's sake?'

So there's the beginning of a plan I think. To Manchester I shall go and I shall go right now. I shall do what I always missed doing when I had familial responsibilities and I shall just go on a whim. If she's not available then I shall spend a day in Manchester.

They must have a couple of decent pubs or some such there if I can't get hold of her?

I shower, shave, put on my best smart-casual-affluent-but-not-totally-smug-middle-aged wealthy-outfit on (if any marketing directors of men's clothing companies are reading this, you can have that brand name for nothing) and head to the station where a puzzled railway employee (with a look that said 'Why would anyone want to go from here to there on a Saturday?') charged me the same, I believe, as a Club Class flight to Abu Dhabi. Thank God money is no longer a problem, I muse.

A paper, a triple-strength espresso and I find a seat in a grubby carriage taking half the child population of Kent to the Science Museum or somewhere. Well better that than taking them to a shopping centre, I muse. At least they're being educated but do they have to be on my train, arguing, fighting, screaming, and eating additive-rich junk food that only increases their ability to argue fight and scream? Should have paid the extra and gone first class.

Still, I resolve to at least try to be tolerant. My kids were once young and misbehaved, I recall. And I wasn't there much for them, in truth.

The coffee's good. I start reading the paper. It appears America's finance system is going to hell in a handcart. Probably a Gucci handcart with diamond inlays, admittedly, but it looks pretty much as if a crash is imminent. Now, obviously as a former CEO of a multi-million dollar business, I must have had a close eye on all the unravellings of the financial market of late. It would have been remiss of me not to.

Truth is, of late I've not really given a flying fuck about the markets (if I ever actually ever did). That was business and I am pretty much extracted from that part of my life and haven't connected it at all to my daily existence. According to these articles, banks might collapse, currency devalue, Wall Street crash in its entirety all over again.

Trouble had been brewing of course. That's what you get if you allow greedy fuckwits to rule the roost in an unregulated bear pit of uncontrolled capitalism. But the rabid reporting from the British media was obviously over the top and designed to terrify all – everyone is doomed, hunter-gatherers only will survive etc. etc. – but most significantly to bring about the fall of the Labour Government. Consequently, wise old sage that I am, I've only spent a little time worrying about all of this. Dilute what you read by about one tenth and you'll get to the truth.

The big events just don't get to me, I am afraid, until afterwards. I never realised I was living through history when the Berlin Wall came down, or Mandela was freed, or Yugoslavia was imploding. It was just the telly. But now you read about these things and realise that what I slept through emotionally, was indeed history.

But I suppose all this might impact on yours truly's new-found fortune.

That's probably what that fuckwit Henry was wanting to talk to me about. He's probably concerned that the returns he promised me (ethical investments only please, obviously) will be diminishing and so with it his fees.

It's all too depressing, all too grown-up. I turn to the back of the paper, pushing thoughts of financial and climactic Armageddon to the corner of my fetid mind, and read the sport, combing the columns for any reference to my formerly beloved Heart of Midlothian.

In truth I don't really care any more about any professional club sport, but I do like to be the only guy in Kent not supporting Manchester United – and so I try to keep up with the passion of my youth if only to stop a footy conversation with blokes dead. ('Who do you support?' 'Hearts.' 'Oh ...' Cue the tumbleweed.)

There's no such information on offer and so, as a sucker for punishment, I read some more about the financial meltdown instead. Would it not, I think, be absolutely typically for good old Jamie, finally with a few bob in his pocket, to lose it all through the incompetence of the global chinless community? Perhaps, given the abuse I've doled out (albeit silently) to those in the financial world, those pesky gods have given with one hand and snatched back, barely able to control their mirth, with the other?

I'd better try to phone Henry, I think. But not now when I'm surrounded by Kent's most feral. I try to sleep for the remaining half hour of the journey to London, but these kids have been well-trained (perhaps by the Chilean secret police) in the subtle art of sleep deprivation. Their screaming mewing and kicking happening all around me keep me awake.

I begin to think about Lizzie.

She was, some thirty years ago, the most upper-class girl I had ever come across. Off-puttingly so: her Home-Counties gymkhana accent grated with me when I first met her. She was just so utterly different from me and to where I came from. Lizzie was, however, very pretty and with, what I would now call, a voluptuous mouth – without really being able to define what that meant without frankly suggesting its involvement in frankly filthy activity. She dressed in a *Country Life*-type way, contrary to the punk look of most of the campus. I found her attractive but obviously unobtainable as by 11 o'clock on an average Friday evening she could usually be found draped across some chinless public school boy Oxbridge reject. So, I admired her from afar, despite myself.

And then one night it just happened. To this day I still do not know how, but we ended up in bed together and virtually stayed there for a term; my chance of achieving anything other than a very ordinary degree all but disappearing, as I learnt from her how to make love properly. God she was fabulous in bed – passionate, giving, lustful and grateful.

We didn't really speak much about important things. I was her Northern 'bit of rough' as she labelled me. I knew little about her family and was certainly never allowed to meet them when they visited. As for what she was going to do after university, she'd laugh when I asked her and say 'Marry well, darling,' and I knew that that would exclude me from her plans. So, we fucked a lot and I was very, very happy with that arrangement.

Until Phil. I went round to her place one afternoon and found her in bed with Phil the rugger bugger and that was it. I drank myself stupid for a couple of weeks. When I saw her and Phil out on campus together, or wrapped around each other in a bar, that would tip me into further drinking myself even stupider. I was hurt, angry – why couldn't she have had the decency to actually end what I thought was a relationship, rather than simply replacing me seemingly overnight with that thick prick son of a landowner? She did try a couple of times to explain, to get me to least talk to her, to 'end it properly', but I had refused.

I got over her eventually. You do at that age. The few male mates I had rallied round, told me I was punching above my weight with Lizzie and that she was a stuck-up poor little rich girl that they'd never actually liked. I got on with life, had a couple of flings, did my finals, got my mediocre degree and launched myself on the world of academic publishing.

And over the years I'd thought of her fleetingly only, until my back-catalogue odyssey had fleetingly thrown us together. We'd nearly gone back to bed ... but didn't. Now she lives in Cheshire with her dull, but wealthy, lawyer husband and continues honing her erotic skills with a variety of meaningless sexual encounters.

She tells me on the occasions that we have met that I am the only person she really engages with emotionally. And I believe her,

Ah Lizzie.

This musing has, I realise disconcertingly, caused trouserly stirrings.

Oh for Christ's sake, every other appendage of my body I can control within reason. I ask you. My genitals just seem to go their own way – possible fans of Fleetwood Mac at their most popular. Always. And this, after the shame-fest of last night. I thought, after the soul-searching and self-analysis, I might be a little more in control of things but no. Unable to sleep, I read more about the financial meltdown.

And so, off the train at Charing Cross and I tube it through London to Euston. My train remarkably is on time and I am shortly speeding through the North London landscape.

I see the impressive building of Alexander Palace on the hill as we shoot past. When I first came to London I lived near here, no, not trendy Muswell Hill but the rough, cheaper side over towards Wood Green. Happy times in a squalid house in a Greek Cypriot area. Now the landscape is filled by shopping malls and endless new housing, apartment blocks with glass and pastel cladding, thousands of them. Who's buying these things?

No one I suspect. Hence the state of the global economy.

Note to self – must phone Henry.

As we head north my phone rings. It's Helen. I let it go to voicemail.

I resist listening to her message.

I decide to text Christine, kind of just for the hell of it. I'm still pretty convinced she mainly attracted to me because of my money and I need that confirmed.

'Thanks for a lovely evening. I enjoyed it hugely,' I type and press send.

Clever. Non-committal. Note no 'x' at the end of the message

I sleep a little, read a bit more of the paper, when the phone rings once more.

It is Christine. I consider ignoring it but I think that churlish. I only texted five minutes ago so she'll know I'm deliberately ignoring her if I don't pick up.

'Christine,' I say quietly, being old-fashioned enough not to expect every other traveller will want to share my conversation. 'How are you?'

'Terrible, actually Jamie. I am so sorry ...'

'Sorry for what?'

'For that stupid fucking kiss of course. What was I thinking?'

I wasn't expecting that.

'Well ... there's nothing to be sorry for. It was a kiss. Actually, a very nice kiss ...' I say this as quietly as possible lest the whole carriage starts listening in to my love life.

Oh fuck, I'm flirting, I realise.

'It was stupid. I was drunk, and you were quite flirty.'

Sorry? I think. It was she that started the eye-gazing nonsense ...

'And I forgot myself and I shouldn't have done and I am very sorry to have put you in that position, especially as things seem to be working out with you and Helen. Though ...' she hesitates then goes on 'you might have mentioned that when we were discussing your marriage. You were a little economic with the truth, I believe ...'

I pause before answering feeling somehow inexplicably that I'm being blamed for something and I'm buggered if I know what. Eventually I parry, 'I didn't say anything only because it is so incredibly complicated and I don't understand what is happening myself. But hang on ... how do you know about ...'

'Because I texted her for your number. And then we talked. I felt awful.'

'Don't feel awful,' I tell her helpfully. 'Look when I get back, let's have a sober lunch and I'll explain.'

'That would be nice. To hear your side, I mean,' she says then adds, 'I never had you down for a cad.' With that she ends the call.

A cad? Me? And who else (but me) uses the C word?

I'm not a little horrified and frankly not a little proud.

We pull into Manchester as I try to unpick what has just happened. So my ex-wife has just told one of her friends, who I inadvertently snogged the night before last, after she hit on me (the friend, not the ex-wife, on this occasion at least ...) that she's cheating on her new but obviously knob-numbingly dull husband with me, her ex-husband.

All quite clear then.

I call Lizzie as I cross the station concourse. It goes straight to her voicemail. I tell her I shall be in the bar of Malmaison at 1 pm precisely.

I'm in there a bit before one. I started on a stroll around Manchester *tout seul*, but it's just kind of sad, a middle-aged bloke in amongst the young families, the young lovers. No, much better and less sad to be a middle-aged bloke in a trendy bar drinking overpriced Pouilly-Fumé on his own.

And the bottle goes as I watch the lunchtime clientele. A couple of hen parties check-in: giggling girls with fake tans, inflatable penises and risqué T-shirts. Then lovers having lunch fresh from a night of illicit passion upstairs.

I look at a couple who take the booth next to me. She's ten years younger than him: lithesome, bottle-blond, slightly nervous. She knows she shouldn't be here – you can tell by the nervous glances around her and the tentative way she grips her wine glass. He's bronzed, white shirt open a little too far. He's a good-looking guy just on the cusp of middle age and therefore decline, but he doesn't need to try quite so hard. But hey, what do I know about anything, me?

He's a lawyer, I surmise, or possibly a banker: wife and two kids in Surrey, guessing from his virtually non-existent accent as he orders champagne. He's not wearing a wedding ring, but you can tell it's been recently removed as there's a white band of skin on the otherwise bronzed finger.

She's his secretary I guess and he's very attentive, lots of touching, lots of whispering and I feel for his wife stuck at home with two young kids whilst her husband is at the conference up North. He's probably now planning on how to make the daily call home to her and what lies he needs to tell to explain a Saturday night away.

Blokes and their libido, anything for a bit of fresh flesh. God I want to hit this guy, I want to tell him the damage he's doing for a quick legover. Why is she, in her relative youth and beauty, interested in you? It's the Porsche, the lifestyle, the champagne, the gifts, the thought that just perhaps she might become wife number two – with the lingering fear that there might be wives three, four and five to content with in the future.

I realise with something approaching a blinding flash that actually I am old-fashioned. Forget the animalistic response to – merged with moralistic disgust of – that awful place I ended up in last night. I do believe in people behaving properly, in doing the right thing. Men need to get a grip and behave with dignity and honesty. Suddenly I believe in chivalrous love. And this guy betrays this belief. I consider telling him to go back to his wife and just grow up.

But I realise, just looking at him, ten years my junior, that my rage is pointless. I can do nothing to change him or anyone else in society. *O tempora, O mores*. And also there's the small matter of my midlife crisis a few years back and the purity of my actions then – and indeed over the last few days. So perhaps the innocent bystander in all this might have a valid case in accusing me somewhat of Himalayan-proportioned hypocrisy.

My phone purrs and I see with some relief that it is Lizzie..

'Dahling,' she says when she's established where I am . 'Change of plan. Come out to the house.' She sounds as if she may have been drinking.

'Won't your husband be there?' I ask naively.

The lawyer/banker overhears this and smiles at me conspiratorially. This is different I think, as I scowl back at him.

'Oh him,' she says. 'No he's playing golf or backgammon or attempting to shag his secretary, poor silly cow. But he wouldn't notice you even if he was here,' she said dismissively.

'See you soon,' I say, with a slight sinking feeling, and she gives me an address.

I hail a cab. 'Posh,' the cabby says when I tell him my desired destination and he trots off the names of a myriad premiership footballers who live round there, only some of whom I have ever heard of.

Out past the sprawling high-rise, run-down housing estates of the suburbs of Manchester. It's becoming like all cities, I muse, where the poor and the troubled are simply removed from the up-market city centres out to lawless *banlieue*. My instinct is to lock the cab door as we pull up at some lights.

A small gang of kids, hoodies up, or faces hidden by baseball caps, gangster roll gaits, the couldn't-care-less way they weave between the stationary cars, daring the passengers to make eye contact. I realise the cabby has central-locked the car anyway in case I do a runner. I must look the sort.

'Rough round here?' I observe conversationally and am then subjected to a ten minute diatribe about immigrants and lazy, druggy kids ruining his once great city, as we leave lower L.A. and hit the Cheshire countryside, out towards Altrincham. And here there are red brick Victorian houses in leafy suburbs, churches, village greens, haberdasheries, artisanal bakers and baristas. This is truly the part of Cheshire that is forever Chiswick.

He turns down a lane of luxury villas, each with massive electronic gates. 'Here you are mate,' he says stopping in front of probably the largest of them.

Christ, it's a mansion. I expect a flunky to appear to open the shabby cab door for me. I pay the guy, turn around and press the buzzer on the entrance system.

The small pedestrian gate clunks open and in I step. I now anticipate wild dogs, Dobermans I imagine, to burst forth from out of the undergrowth that shelters the gravel path from gate to house. Now we're talking sizable undergrowth here, wide and deep enough to hide multiple Dobermans, wildebeest, zebra and Thomson's gazelle. Dr Livingston himself would have taken days to traverse this terrain. Mercifully I walk the five hundred meters to the front door over reassuringly crunchy gravel, without being torn to shreds or trampled upon.

The door opens and Lizzie is standing there. Looking, I have to say rather lovely. She is wearing tight, dark jeans and a simple white blouse, with a bold expensive necklace that's properly worth more than the cabby earns in two years. She has high-priced, high-heeled boots on that, not terribly surprisingly, make her seem taller. She'd still be recognisable in a large crowd as Lizzie from university.

She has a saucy smile on her face. We hug, her body pushed against mine.

'Welcome, dahling,' she purrs, 'to the house of fun. Drink?'

I step into a baronial if, I have to say, rather vulgar hallway. Lots of horse images – oil paintings, pottery, bronzes. She sees I am looking and says 'Geoffrey's obsession. Spends a fortune on the fucking things. Won at Aintree earlier this season,' she says disparagingly of a photograph of three white, middle-aged blokes, one presumably Geoffrey, in top hats and tails patting a grey thoroughbred. 'Keeps him out of my hair, though.'

We move into a kitchen that is bigger than the food hall at Harrods. She opens the wine fridge. 'Here's one I started earlier,' she says, laughing, picking out a bottle. She gets a clean glass out of a cupboard, picks up a half-full one on the side, quaffs the contents down in one and then fills both. She opens another cupboard and tosses the empty bottle into a box that contains a dozen or so such empties.

'Let's relax,' she says passing me the glass. We clink.

She takes me out to a conservatory that presumably was built to house a Great Exhibition. Huge. It backs onto vast grounds, undulating mounds of lawn, mature trees, a lake with a rowing boat tethered, and ducks and moorhen bobbing gently.

'Jesus Lizzie,' I say, 'This place ... it's massive.' This level of wealth makes me feel as if I've just found a tenner in Tesco's car park.

'Oh fuck off darling,' she says. 'It's ostentatious and it's cold and it's sterile and it's boring ...' she sobs a little 'and I am fucking cold and sterile and bored out of my tiny little skull living here.' And she starts to cry.

Now, I know Lizzie. Fickle sexually as a teenage student, she's was openly fickle sexually in married adulthood revelling in the little passionate – affairs is the wrong word, more flings or intrigues – with a seemingly vast array of local men from the gardener to a couple of former Premiership football players. She had always been open with me about this, and I had always assumed she was happy with her lot.

But here in the glare of a northern late-summer afternoon, she just looks old and tired. She finishes her glass, goes out towards the kitchen slightly unsteadily returning with an open full bottle from which she pours herself another. She offers me one, but I have barely touched my first glass.

She's obviously quite pissed.

'I thought you loved all this,' I said.

'I did. Or at least I thought I did. But I realise that I have no one to grow old with. Sure, there are plenty of blokes who'd happily hook up with me for a fuck.' She sobs again. 'I'm sorry. You must think I'm a frightful mess but I was feeling low today and started on the Pouilly a little earlier than usual.' She took another swig and lit a cigarette blowing the smoke forcibly out and continuing, 'Then you called and I felt happy again. How does that work then Jamie?'

'Oh Lizzie, I don't know,' I say pathetically. Thinking, I came here for help and advice from the one person who seemed to have life at least partially sorted and now look at the mess I appear to be in. 'I don't know, 'I say again for want, frankly, of anything more insightful to say.

'I do,' she says, standing up then positioning herself right beside me. 'I do.' I am struck momentarily by the thought that I am actually in some am-dram Pinter play such are the dynamics of the dialogue, but she goes on, 'We, you and me, should be together. We always should have been. I mean, I screwed up big time all those years ago in letting you go.' And with that she went to kiss me.

13. Slow Train Coming

What the fuck, Dear Reader, is going on? Please, someone, somewhere, cast light on the tragic-comedy that is my current life.

Fact 1) I'm a middle-aged bloke in not bad condition considering I'm on the SAGA mailing list – but I'm certainly more likely to be mistaken for George Galloway than Clooney. I mean I'm fair-to-middling in looks, personality and personal hygiene, but I'm self-aware enough to know my limitations.

Fact 2) The major difference between the me of five years back and the me of now, is that the Tooth Fairy for some inexplicable reason has chosen to pop a few million – some would say undeservedly, and I would not argue against that viewpoint – quid under my pillow while soundly I slumbered.

Fact 3) Seemingly up until three weeks ago, to have been snogged by any sentient being would have meant me either committing atrocities during the night at the local Cheshire Home or hitting Portsmouth Docks with a pocket full of tenners.

Fact 4) I seem to have turned into a middle-aged babe magnet (no, I have to get this right, that should read a magnet for middle-aged babes) virtually overnight.

Fact 5) None of this is making me happy. All of this conspires to make me uneasy, mildly depressed, slightly resentful but above all absolutely utterly one hundred per cent fucking confused.

I'm on the train now as it draws out of Manchester Piccadilly and I feel nothing short of relief. As it gathers momentum and the cityscape of south Manchester comes in to view, my cares seems to lift a little as I am pulled away from the small ball of albeit voluptuous trouble that was dear old Lizzie. Oh lordie, how I suffer for my art. Whatever that may be.

I managed to stop her trying to kiss me. I was on the cusp of telling l her I had just recovered from herpes, but actually she calmed down a little when I offered to pour her another glass of her mother's little helper from the Loire. And as that only released enough to fill half a glass, I then had to dig out another bottle from the fridge, and then find a user manual for the Heath Robinson-esque corkscrew (obviously expensive and presumably from Harvey Nicks but utterly useless at screwing corks compared to a two quid screw and twist Tesco's job) that she had so easily mastered. But at least that deflected the immediate carnality that seemed to be uppermost in her mind. I then managed to nearly cut the top of my finger off on the little pen knife that flicked open inexplicably (apparently, I was meant to use it to take the foil off the top of the bottle) so I swore profusely and fluently and feigned near death (silently noting that the retirement career option of concert pianist was now under severe threat) – a distraction tactic that actually worked because by the time she'd found a plaster and the bleeding was stemmed and the blood mopped up off the Welsh slate mine that had been emptied to supply her kitchen floor, she'd stopped trying to stick her sozzled mouth over mine.

I managed to sit her back down in the conservatory that now reminded me for all the world of a drained aquarium for blue whales, and got her to talk. Well, we actually had a bit of a cuddle and a laugh about the fact that the fates were conspiring to keep us from exchanging bodily fluids this time through my near bleeding to death (OK, I exaggerate a bit but it was quite a deep cut, OK? And those little knives are very sharp, actually ...).

Anyway she talked and we drank. I had some catching up to do plonk-wise and I figured if I drank speedily from her stash then it may be doing her a favour by reducing her supply but it wasn't to be. Her fridge was massive, like some sort of walk-in mortuary compartment designed as a one-off by a white goods' consumer company. It appeared to contain about fifty more bottles of the stuff.

She talked. And she talked some more. About her unfulfilled life, about her decaying mind, about her crap marriage, about her dull husband and this footballer's wife's house she rattled around in – where she was surrounded, not surprisingly, by footballers' wives. Some memorable quotes flew from her. 'The last time I had a real original thought, Duran Duran were the next big thing.' 'The last decent orgasm I had was courtesy of Ann Summers and the Duracell stolen from the TV remote control.' It just flowed this self-awareness, this slight despair, but underpinned by her innate humour. I realised that the more she was drinking the more sober, the more lucid, and the more insightful, she was becoming.

She became almost sanguine about the wrong choices she'd made. 'I actually qualified as a solicitor,' she reminded me. I'd forgotten that all those years ago at university she somehow managed to squeeze in the study of some law, in-between cheating on me with the landowning, utterly chinless rugger bugger that was Phil. (I repeat, I am over Phil by the way. What might make you think otherwise ...?)

OK, I'm lying. When forced to recall that day I am still filled with shock and dread. Me finding my then beloved *in flagrante delicto* with one so dulled by his minor public school education as to not even be able to recognise the language of that phrase as being Latin, let alone understanding what it meant. I mean, I think I could have coped with being cuckolded if only by someone who had read Tacitus. But I'm over it, OK?

'Yup, got a job in Geoffrey's,' (her now hubby's) 'business, and actually was doing rather well. Then the grubby little bastard started paying attention to my briefs as much as his clients' and that, as they say, was that.'

I hadn't heard this story before and I was intrigued. 'Why would you allow a grubby little bastard anywhere near your briefs?' I asked her, genuinely intrigued.

'Oh come on Jamie, don't be dim,' she snorted. 'He was a senior partner. He had a Porsche that would become his second car when his Ferrari was delivered; he liked nice restaurants and good hotels and he spoiled me and bought me jewellery; and told me he'd look after me and, I was – if not exactly smitten – then I was totally ensnared by the certain knowledge that this man would be able to look after me for the rest of my life. Then his wife found out.'

'His wife?' I blurted out. God I'm just so old fashioned sometimes ...

'Oh didn't I mention her? Dreadful ugly old thing, who according to Geoffrey, was dried up and shrivelled in all the places you don't want a woman to be dried up and shrivelled. Nope, she found out about us by sitting in the bar of a swanky hotel in Manchester,' (I feel certain it's the one I was in earlier but I cannot bring myself to ask) 'and confronting us as we came downstairs after a peculiarly unspectacular bonk. A bloody divorce ensued. Oh and then I had a miscarriage. Often wonder what would have happened had I had kids.'

She lit a cigarette and took a drink and stared into middle distance out across the arboretum that was her garden, and I knew she was thinking of a house with the smell and noise of children. 'At least I would have had some comfort in my old age.'

There was a silence and I didn't know what to say. Various platitudes – oh, it's not too late to find happiness: you could adopt children, do charity work, write a book: all the stuff that you're meant to trot out in hopeless situations like this where you know nothing that you say or do will make any difference – sprung to mind but remained unspoken. This was Lizzie here. She can spot bullshit at a hundred yards as she's lived her life knee-deep in it.

Some people, it seems to me, are beyond redemption. Offer her the choice – if she could have her time again: of a fulfilling career but with a household budget to stick to, a five-year-old family Citroën and a three-bed semi in a suburb; or what she has now – and she, I suspect, would take the latter every time. She's been hotwired from birth for the life she leads.

Let's be honest, she'd probably have been a hopeless mother, self-obsessed and more than likely jealous of her children's youth, and definitely farming out the more demanding element of child-rearing to a nanny. Not because she's a bad person but because that would be learned behaviour from her own mother.

And then I remembered the conversation I'd had with Christine over the curry and it struck me. It was Lizzie's comment about being looked after for the rest of her life that resonated. That's what some women of my generation still wanted. They were genetically programmed to be cared for, to be supplied by their man with the things that apparently make life bearable. Not love, not affection, not companionship: *Things*. And please note before you bundle me into that big box marked Sexist Old Bastard, I'm talking some women here, not mercifully all.

I think it must be a throwback to the post-war generation. My mother was an intelligent woman, had a good job, married a lovely man and exchanged paid employment (seemingly willingly) for a twin-tub and a housecoat. That was understandable. That was the austere post-war fifties. But why did at least some of the offspring of that generation – who went through the huge social change of the sixties, then (you can virtually forget the first six years of the seventies), the punk and post-punk politics that exploded afterwards when I was at university – why and how did the man-as-provider mantra still survive? Supposedly smart women of my age – and some younger – still like men with dosh.

Women like Lizzie betray their sex by being blessed with intelligence and not using it. My mind strayed back to the private school my kids went to, and the assortment of yummy mummies I'd occasionally mingle with, if I was tasked with doing a school run. There were a lot of clever, educated women there married to accountants, estate agents or merchant bankers – obviously neo-Nazis to a fucking man – who should have known better than to let their brains disappear whilst shopping with their old man's credit card and obsessing about their Pilates classes.

Am I the one being sexist? If a woman chooses that life then surely that's her right? Who am I to judge ...? Good on her, you might say. But somehow for me it just doesn't seem right.

And so on, the ever-contradicting dilemma of being a man and trying to park the sexist impregnation that is the result of growing up in the sixties and seventies.

As Lizzie kept lamenting her lot – now on the subject of her bitchy female friends – I continued to muse through the booze. I needed out of there I realised; this was not the counselling session I had in mind.

The train is now carving through the Cheshire countryside. I see Mow Cop on the distant hill and momentarily recollect walks with friends there nearly forty years ago – I was at what laughingly passed for a university near here. I stop myself (through surprising willpower) from reminiscing further. I remind myself that I've done to death the retracing of my past and look where that had got me. I must look forward, only forward.

And Lizzie is behind me in every sense. I won't meet her again – it's just too painful to see someone wasting their life. I know in ten years' time she'll still be booze-fuddled and unhappy, finding occasional affairs harder to come by as her body and beauty disappear into genuine old age. Maybe she'll even resort to buying in the services of some gigolo, a sad thought. No, I shall break with her as I cannot help her.

But she's helped me a little, though. I have realised that my current situation vis-à-vis Helen at least is, disappointingly, probably the result of money (I'm less sure about Christine being a part of my money-grabbing-women theory by the way – maybe she just liked me ...). Yup it is sad to have to admit it to myself. There was me thinking that it was my wit and energy and middle-aged good looks that were responsible for the sudden lack of a shitty stick big enough to keep these woman away – but now I have to face up to the fact that I am only a babe magnet because I, for the first time, have money.

What to do with this sudden realisation? I don't know, truly. Perhaps just understanding the circumstances is enough and I don't need to do anything? Perhaps I cynically take advantage of it and go on an admittedly sad, middle-aged shag fest? Well, no. That's not me is it, I'm far too decent for that, even if I say it myself.

And then as the train pulls into Stoke-on-Trent I begin to feel a bit of a naïf, a bit of a fool. All this stuff to do with women was happening around me and I just didn't see it. I didn't appreciate why it was happening. I thought I was streetwise and all along I've been what can only be described as mildly rather dim.

Good. I know now.

I go the buffet car and get a couple of miniature bottles of wine that pro rata cost about the same as a moderate bottle of Château Lafitte – truly the second Great Train Robbery. After all, Lizzie's wine is starting to wear off. I allow myself to obsess for a couple of minutes about this corporate theft as it relieves me of my darker mood.

The first little bottle disappears in a couple of gulps, and I feel mild drunkenness returning once more. And with it, some self-realisation.

I've got it now, I think. I go home and I immerse myself in something new. I do need a purpose in my life. It might be charity work; I might set up a business; I may go on a journey or invest. Something. I'm not going to go back to being chased by women and there's a sentence I never thought I'd ever have the opportunity to utter.

Decided. Sorted. Done and indeed dusted. My life for the next few months if not years. Uncomplicated, clear, useful, meaningful and purposeful.

I get the paper out that I bought and skim-read earlier today and feel a warm comfort. Lizzie has helped after all. She's sorted out my head a little, as her own became increasingly pickled, and I raise a glass to her. If she wants a gigolo let her have one. That I guess is empowerment.

My mobile chirrups and I take it out of my pocket. I don't recognise the number, but I see it's an Edinburgh one and so intrigued I answer it.

'Jamie?' a precise cool, Scottish voice says calmly. 'It's Kathlyn here. David's wife. I'm sorry to say but David is dead.'

I stare out of the window, the phone held to my ear, unable to compute or indeed respond to the words I've just heard. My reaction? A strangled 'Fuck.'

14. Buckets of Rain

It was a massive stroke she told me when I managed to reply to her properly, and it had happened on the squash court. He was declared dead within an hour.

'He'd have wanted you to know immediately Jamie. He always counted you as one of his dearest and oldest friends. He loved and trusted you.'

Shit, I thought, did he? I'd not been in much contact with him since I'd seen him on my retro road trip of a few years ago. He loved and trusted me? Can't have had many mates then in the banking halls of Edinburgh.

'The funeral is next Wednesday', she told me, 'and it would mean a lot to the family if you could attend. Maybe do a reading? We'd all like that.' She was so calm, as if she was inviting me over for a light supper. Calm or cold? I asked myself and could not decide.

'Of course, I'll be there,' I said.

'Please,' she said, 'stay at the house. I think you'll be some comfort to the children, they're obviously devastated.' I thanked her, trying to work out how old David's kids must be. Mid-teens, I guessed. There then followed ten or so minutes of dodgy reception as the train went through tunnels. I told her I'd call her as soon as possible when I was home to discuss arrangements.

I drank the second bottle of wine virtually in one go. David, dead. David – who I'd known since I was about five years of age. David – whose sporting talent, good looks, keen brain, lucrative job and pools of charm had made him just a teensy bit of a thorn in my side for nearly forty-five years. He was just so ... blessed. The pretty Edinburgh lawyer wife, the single-figure golf handicap, the ability to glide through life successfully and seemingly effortlessly.

When I'd last seen him on my road trip around Britain, the evening eventually had descended into serious and disgusting drunkenness. Then came the confession and contrition from David – but the thing I do remember most was the elation that I felt when I saw him in that bar for the first time in about twenty years. The golden youth was suffering from severe baldness and that, shallow bastard that I am, had made my heart soar. I'd tried to restrain myself of course from mentioning it and had successfully made no reference to it for what ... at least two or three minutes into the meeting.

The evening became somewhat Bacchanalian when we met, by chance, his dirty wee secret in the shape of the shapely Alison. And then he'd poured it all out. He, loyal father, husband and Kirk Elder, who had never before strayed from the path of righteousness and temperance in the trouser department, had fallen for the charms of a beautiful woman twenty years his junior. I remember telling him that it happens, whilst thinking, somewhat churlishly, that it never fucking happens to me.

Kathlyn had made him pay. Yes, she took him back eventually, but full forgiveness was never on the cards. His life had become a difficult one. There was a permafrost coldness about the relationship that he recognised was the result of his betrayal, and he had even accepted he deserved it. But he had expressed concern about how long it might last. 'Surely she can't make me pay for the rest of my life? What's the point in staying together if we're both so unhappy?' I remember him asking me when we were on about our fourth bottle of wine.

David's dead. Sitting there as the train pulled into Birmingham it just seemed impossible. David, fit and clean-living (at least pre-Alison), dead.

I realise this is the first death of a friend and contemporary that I've had to experience. Parents, well that's a terrible loss to deal with and often compounded by feelings of ingratitude and guilt ('I could/should have done more for them') both emotionally and practically – but from the moment you achieve some self-realisation and awareness you know that at some time in the future you'll be facing life without those very people who brought you into it and nurtured you subsequently. There's a grinding inevitability that you'll one day be orphaned. It happened to me at a relatively young age, and it hurt and it still hurts. You go for days without thinking of them and then suddenly a memory, or a face in a crowd, or an expression or a dream even, takes you tumbling back to the rock face of loss and despair. But that's the way of the world. The elderly die. Dying when you're fit and relatively young and clean-living shouldn't be the way of the world.

And then there's the stuff she'd told me about how David viewed our friendship. Fuck, I think, I didn't even realise I was that close a friend to him. I mean he was part of my quest to discover who I was through trying to meet everyone I ever knew and that had kindled a friendship of sorts. Perhaps, in his prim and proper world of international banking, the Kirk and the golf club, his friendship base was such that he couldn't enjoy a bottle of wine to himself and talk about his sexual guilt. Maybe I was part-mate, part-confessor?

Perhaps that was it. Maybe I was his only true friend and I simply didn't realise it.

At New Street I consider momentarily getting off this train and heading up to Edinburgh direct from there. But that would be pointless as I obviously would have no luggage. But something is compelling me to go back to Edinburgh.

I spend the rest of the train journey trying to analyse my response to this latest drama (well, tragedy, actually). I have a long-held theory that blokes have relationships with other blokes (I'm talking non-sexual here by the way) that are fundamentally underpinned by rivalry and competitiveness.

So, you'll have a mate whose company you like and who you've been able to hugely enjoy meeting up with once a month for a hundred years (oh Reader, please don't be so literal ...) and who is your best and closest friend.

You'd do anything for him excluding criminality or sexual services. OK, he's more successful than you, in that he earns twice what you do (the only valid way of judging success apparently in these Thatcher-legacy days I believe). He's got an extraordinarily pretty wife and two kids at expensive public schools. But he's fun and he's funny and he's well-balanced and he's not at all up himself and he drinks to excess and you enjoy, indeed, look forward to, your once-a-month night out. He's the only person on God's earth that you'd share nearly any secret with, as you'd trust him with your life.

He loses his job. Or one of his kids ends up pregnant. Or his perfect wife leaves him for a lesbian trawler captain (maybe all three of those at once – you'd get great odds at the bookies on that, granted). He's devastated and you're there to help him through, to support him, to drink his Scotch whilst he pours out the pain and the disappointment, the self-regret and the blame. You're there to reassure him, to tell him that this is not of his doing, that bad things happen to good people and that he'll come through it stronger and better.

But look into your heart. There's a tiny part of you that's saying 'Yes! I beat the bastard ...' because it's not your wife being tossed (literally and metaphorically) on the North Sea, nor is it your kid that's about to give birth at the age of sixteen, and you still have your, albeit underpaid, employment.

It's subliminal. You barely admit it even to yourself, but other's pain brings just a crumb of self-satisfaction. And it doesn't alter how you behave towards him. Of course, you'll still be the best friend you can possibly be, but that slight feeling will still niggle away at you that secretly, deep down, you're just a wee bit pleased at his misery.

And the worst part of it all? Your hurting friend, he knows what you're feeling because he'd feel the same if the roles were reversed.

And there's a not a little of this strangely, nay perversely – going through my head on this interminable journey across London and down through Kent. I'm sad he's died. Tomorrow when it truly sinks in, I'll be devastated he's died.

It was like that night in Edinburgh four or five years back when his dirty laundry spilled out through our meeting with Alison (and believe me there's barely a bloke with a pulse who wouldn't consider soiling his laundry with the likes of Alison). He was in pain, he was racked with guilt at his lust and betrayal. He was worried about his social standing and his career if his indiscretion (his only ever indiscretion I believe) got out. And I was there to support him and to listen and to tell him that he wasn't a bad man and that these things do happen.

I was good that night. I was a friend. I was possibly his only friend that he could unburden himself upon. And yes I was genuine in my advise and desire to support him. I meant it – I shared his pain.

But also, I have to confess that I had enjoyed that slight feeling of superiority over him. Obviously that evening had begun rather pathetically on my part when I saw his balding pate shining in the bar room lights, and I had to prove a point by sweeping my own tumbling locks back rakishly. But then as the evening unfolded, I'd felt smug that my life, terrible as it was at the time, wasn't the total fucking twenty-car pile-up on the M9 just past Grangemouth that his was.

And now the man I'd known nearly all my life was dead and my petty jealousies just seem so unbecoming. I feel a little ashamed, but I have beaten him just this once by still being alive.

15. Things Have Changed

The next day I awake with a once again familiar hangover. Of course, when I'd got in last night – still shocked and somewhat guilty at what my psyche had revealed – I wrapped myself around a bottle of the best thing to come off the Island of Jura. That plus the bath full of wine I'd consumed at Lizzie's and on the train (oh the Marks and Sparks was still open at Charing Cross so I'd filled up there for the difficult hour-long trip out of London) meant that I was feeling far from clear-headed or indeed fragrant.

I make a note to myself. I've deteriorated of late, revisiting my previous alcohol dependency of a few years back and that wasn't, nor indeed isn't, a good thing. I need to get it under control again. And I will, once the funeral is over.

I've a plan. I'm going to take the shiny new motor out of the garage tomorrow and head north. I shall stop off on route, I shall revisit a couple of places I recall going to with my parents that I haven't been to for years. It will be a gentle saunter up the east coast. I shall stay somewhere nice in York, walk the fair streets of that fine city, and then the next day amble through the wilds of Northumberland and the Scottish borders. It sounds idyllic. I shall be on my own with my thoughts and the digital Bee Gee-free radio (I can only hope) and away from Helen and away from Christine.

Today, however, I'm taking Ailsa for lunch. I text her to ask where she'd like to go and if Nick would be joining us. 'You've woken me up!' is all I get from her back.

I check the house phone and Helen has left four messages suggesting dinner. She can, I think wittily, fuck right off for the next few days at least. I send her a short text. 'David's dead. I am off to his funeral. Will call you when I get back.'

She rings me back virtually immediately. I ignore it.

I start to pack quickly. I find the darkest suit I own and quickly run an iron over it. I can't find a black tie so I head out to buy one as soon as the shops are open. I pack enough clothes for four or five days and end up with a bag that frankly looks to big to fit in the dwarf's car that I've just spent good money on. Something to worry about tomorrow morning, I think, imagining myself driving to Edinburgh, the roof down all the way and my bag strapped in beside me on the passenger seat.

Ailsa deigns to respond at about 11.30. She suggests a pizza restaurant at 12.30.

I'm seated waiting for her when she arrives ten minutes late. I've ordered a bottle of red. I go to kiss her and she proffers her cheek reluctantly. 'Don't worry,' I say. 'No one knows you in here,' as she takes her seat.

'How would you know Dad?' she replies. 'bet you thought no one knew you when you were snogging your girlfriend at the station?'

She smirks as she says this.

'She's not my girlfriend. She's a friend of your mother's ...'

Before I can reflect upon the failed tactics of this response, she's on to me like a lioness on a slight lame gazelle.

'Do you snog all of Mum's friends, Dad?' Deadpan. Ice cool. Impressive.

'Actually, Nick was quite impressed,' she continues. 'Thought your girlfriend ...' she waves away my weary attempt at an objection ... 'was a bit of a yummy mum.'

'Look,' I say, 'It wasn't as it seemed. We're just friends, really.'

'Friends don't stick their tongues down each other's throats..'

'Ailsa!' I say. 'Do not be so coarse.' I hear my mother's voice using those self-same words to me forty years back.

'Dad,' she says, 'if you can be so judgemental about Nick, I can be the same about you and the mystery babe.'

Discretion and valour spring to mind here. I take a deep breath then say, 'I apologise for being judgemental, Ailsa. Now, can we start again and just enjoy lunch together?'

'Apology accepted,' she says, a little smugly for a seventeen-year-old, I feel. She studies the menu. 'But you have to promise to stop the cigarettes. Really. I don't want a dead dad during my A levels.'

I exhale loudly utterly defeated and say, 'I promise. Next time you see me, I'll be an ex-smoker. Truly.'

'OK,' she says. 'You'd better stick to that, Dad, OK? Oh, can I have some wine?'

'No, you bloody can't!' I say. 'It's illegal – you're only seventeen!'

'Christ Dad, you're more boring than Edward ...'

That hurts, I can tell you.

'Anyway,' she says. 'I'm allowed a drink if I'm eating with a responsible adult. You probably qualify ...'

I let her have a glass of wine, ignoring her deadpan jibe and unsure if she's just made that particular bit of legislation up.. But she looks like she's in her early twenties anyway, and the staff don't challenge her.

'Sorry about your friend,' she then says, a little awkwardly. I'm surprised not only that she's mature enough to address the difficult subject of death straight on, but also that she knows.

I smile what I think is wryly and say, 'Thank you. Sad. But these things happen when you get to my age. How did you know?'

'Mum told me as I was leaving.'

That makes sense, I thought, but still feeling a little stalked.

We order food, and settle into a real conversation. She tells me about school, her friends, her teachers, pleasant tittle-tattle and I'm feeling good about things. She's fond of Nick but neither of them want anything serious. 'We're too young,' she says. 'We both want fun at uni.' We're talking effortlessly and enjoying each others' company. I'm like a real dad, I think, a little smugly.

She'd always been a good linguist, a natural at French. I ask her what A levels she's planning to do assuming, an array of Humanities.

'Maths, Economics and History,' she says.

'Oh!' I say, which is obviously not the response she was wanting.

'What's wrong?' she asks.

'Nothing,' I say. 'Nothing at all. I'm just ... a little surprised. I thought, you know, English, French, maybe another language...? You were always such a good linguist. You loved reading ...'

'I won't get onto an Economics course at anywhere good without Maths and Economics, Dad. And I can read when I'm not working.'

I slightly choke on my garlic dough ball. 'I didn't know you wanted to study Economics,' I reply.

'How else am I going to get into banking?' she asks me as if I am truly the stupidest person she's ever met.

I try to cover my surprise. 'Banking ... that's er ... very well-paid ... excellent idea.'

'Mum said you'd disapprove.'

'I don't disapprove, Ailsa, truly.' She looks at me in an unbelieving manner. 'Truly I don't. Someone's got to do it. If it had been reinsurance, then I would have disapproved.' A poor joke, I accept, but it diffused the situation a wee bit. 'What did your Mum say, precisely?'

'Oh just that you're an old lefty.'

'Guilty,' I say.

'A sad old lefty who can be ... just a bit of a hypocrite.' She sips some wine after saying that. 'sorry Dad. That was a bit brutal.'

'Not at all,' I say, stung by the brutality. But you'll learn,' I'm using what I hope is my most sage voice, 'everyone's a hypocrite. I comes with being an adult.' I'm trying to deflect this attack on my moral standing. 'And when did she say this about me?'

'She's been saying it really ever since you split up. A champagne socialist, she calls you.'

'That's original. But I am guilty as charged. I like nice things. I just don't believe the people who provide the nice things are properly rewarded. And they should be. That's all.'

'You haven't told her about the money.' She looks at me deadpan.

Fuck. The world, his auntie and his seventeen former wives all seem to know about my money

I exhale, take a slug of wine, and then empty the remains of the bottle into my glass and say, 'Ailsa, honey, it's none of her business, truly. I provide. I will provide for you and Cameron. I've just got lucky.'

'She said yesterday she'd never have left you if she'd known you'd be rich.'

I stop eating and look at my daughter. Why is she saying these things?

'Ailsa, she left me because I was a horrible person and because the marriage was over. Done. She has Edward. He provides. It's the best thing that happened to her, truly.'

'It wasn't the best thing for Cameron and me, though. Did either of you consider that?' she says, tears in her eyes. Her glass is empty and without hesitating she picks up mine and swallows half of it in one. 'At least you could be fun. Living in Edward's house, it's like a mausoleum. Now you've money ... couldn't you and Mum think about getting back together?'

***

The rest of the lunch passed in something of a daze, I have to say.

We said goodbye, an embarrassed peck on the cheek from me outside the restaurant as we went our separate ways.

As I walked back to my flat, I felt ... foolish. It was pretty obvious I'd been targeted, not by Ailsa – she was just saying what she felt – but so obviously by Helen. Had that shopping centre meeting that proved to be the catalyst for much extra-ex-marital carnality, been somehow planned? I'd been entrapped by set of new breasts and that, if nothing else, is a tribute to my shallowness.

What of Ailsa? Had both kids really been so cut up by our splitting up? If so, how the fuck was it I hadn't noticed? Why didn't Helen tell me? I could have been...just better, more caring, attentive. But I'd assumed everyone was adult enough to recognise that the split was the for the best.

I stop on the way home – yes, you've guessed it, old friend – at the off-licence. Back at the flat, the wine erases some of the anger, some of the hurt. I send a text to Ailsa thanking her for coming for lunch with me. I get an 'xx' in return, a better sign of love from her than I probably deserve.

The phone rings. It's Helen. I let it go to voicemail. I need to properly work out what I think she has been doing and I'm not going to speak to her until I've done so.

But five minutes later, I succumb to temptation and listen to her message. Where I learn that, apparently I've upset Ailsa and I need to rectify that quickly. She wishes me a safe journey.

I fall into a somewhat troubled slumber.

16. Road to Nowhere

Awake, surprisingly refreshed, I head out to the car. A road trip, I think with a degree of excitement, and then immediately feel a bit guilty about taking pleasure from this particular set of circumstances. I'd barely thought of David in the last twenty-four hours as I had been so wrapped up in my own little drama. But I go a little easy on myself by acknowledging that I am going to end up not only mourning my friend, but helping his family to cope with their bereavement. There will be people there to talk with, to enjoy their company and who will benefit from my compassion and, I hope, my wisdom. And I shall revisit a couple of old haunts, and those old haunts shall be free of the people I used to enjoy them with.

And they shall be free of the huntress and temptress, Helen.

I'm done with that looking for old flames and old friends. I did that spectacularly badly five years ago and look where it got me. A lot of scrapes, no little humiliation, sclerosis and a mugging from a mad Christian. Oh and a new job that turned out pretty well for me, and a split marriage that actually turned out pretty well for me too – although I've since learnt that, apparently, my children's lives have been ruined as a result.

I'm off to York first, a city I love. I've booked a nice hotel and will meander through the medieval city centre, dine well and then continue my journey the next day. It's a plan, it's a tad self-indulgent but hey, sometimes a fellow just has to indulge himself.

I manage to open the boot of the car eventually only to then realise the bag I want it to carry is too big. In fact, any bag in this boot would be too big unless you're a fucking dwarf. I'm actually wondering if they've swapped the glove compartment for the boot in some perverse German designer's joke, but then I kind of get it. These wee sports cars aren't meant for serious journeys where you might actually want to take some luggage. Lord no.

I realise with a sinking heart that this car is not money well spent.

I shove the case on the back seat and hit the road and in seemingly no time at all I am on the outskirts of York. It's a dully uneventful journey. I find the hotel I'm after, which is in a quaintly old-fashioned townhouse overlooking the river.

I check in and then go for a walk.

I remember this place from a school trip when we were supposed to explore the Castle Museum but instead six of us bought several cans of lager and sat by the Ouse all day getting slowly sozzled. I remember that day feeling properly accepted for the first time by my classmates. Don't forget, I'd been parachuted at fourteen from Edinburgh to Teesside and that was not an easy time for yours truly. These people thought folk from Durham were strangely exotic, so when I turned up as lanky git with a Scottish accent the drawbridge was up against the foreign invaders. It took me some considerable time to make friends and it caused me, I am certain, to be rather shy and withdrawn in my early adulthood.

York had been a turning point. I was accepted by the cool kids at last. The acceptance was partly facilitated by me being the one with a tenner in his pocket and the balls to actually go and buy the beers, but I felt that a price worth paying.

And then my parents moved again, this time to a small town ten miles south of York. This was in my first year at university and so, during long summer holidays I was on my own. Then in the Easter holiday of my final year I spent time allegedly revising at the library at York University.

As I walk down the Shambles past the throngs of tourists I have a memory of those times. Of being in the library and seeing a stunning girl. And catching her eye and looking away embarrassed. I knew when a girl was out of my league. I looked up again and she was looking at me once more. I looked away.

I got up to browse through some obscure journals on poetry in order to steal some original thoughts for my Virgil essay when suddenly she was five feet away from me at the same shelves. Diffidently, my heart tearing itself out of its casing I took a sideways step towards her. She did the same towards me.

My keen intellect picked up that she was doing this deliberately. She obviously wanted me to engage. I stood there staring ahead, this vision but two feet away from me ... and I bottled it.

I bottled it. I wracked my brains for something to say to her and knew that whatever I tried would make me sound like a moron and so I took a journal, any fucking journal, and with self-hatred burning, I turned my back on her and I sat back down at my desk. The vision had packed her bag without looking at me again and left. I considered doing the same chasing her, suggesting a drink, a coffee, something, anything ... but I didn't.

I saw her two days later on this self-same street; I'm standing on now with two friends. She glanced at me and as I passed, I heard laughter. I knew I was the object of that laughter and I burned with shame.

Don't get me wrong, as previously recounted I had had my share of undergraduate flings but they were always the result of intoxication from some source or other. Well, strictly speaking, very often intoxication from many different sources in the course of the same evening. Lizzie – until she simultaneously spoilt her copybook and student bedding with Phil de Wiltshire – was one relationship that started with a dance-floor fumble and ended up in months of slavish devotion, on my part at least.

But no, in that Heslington library was a gorgeous, sober woman who made it very obvious that she wanted me to engage with her. And I didn't. I didn't because I was shy and awkward and embarrassed, but most of all I didn't because I was stone-cold sober and I didn't do sober very well at that time. Still not great at it now.

I pay my twelve pounds to get into the Minster. If I wasn't so self-absorbed I'd object to this ridiculous charge, but I don't because I'm well ... self-absorbed. Forget the bollocks earlier of the weekend about thinking too much and isolation being bad for me – I love this stuff. I love the cod self-analysis and, who knows, it might even eventually sort me out mentally.

I wander the medieval splendour. I'm treading in the footsteps of the Emperor Constantine (well strictly speaking about fifty feet above his footsteps but leave the archaeological pedantry to me please). I see the heart of Yorkshire in the stained glass windows and I stroll, stroll like an anonymous tourist amongst the other anonymous – but I have to say fucking noisy – tourists.

I wish I did God. I envy people that do. To them this mighty building, this huge political statement about Christianity and the Church, must inspire not just the mind (it certainly inspires mine) but the soul too. I can revel in the artistry, I can imagine the awe of the people of the city as this structure was thrown up towards the heaven in which they were certain their god was present. I wonder how many of the workmen died falling from mediaeval scaffolding. Fast-tracked straight to heaven I assume, given the privileged location of their demise.

A few people are in the chapels off to the side, praying devoutly, genuflecting. Do they have to pay their twelve quid too? I muse. Fuck of a lot for the privilege of prayer. Maybe the simple act of paying for their spiritual place here makes them feel closer to their god. I'm not mocking them. As I say, I envy people with that degree of certainty. Life must be so very simple if you know what the point of it is.

Down to the crypt to walk properly in Constantine's footsteps (bloody pedant) and to see parts of the Roman town. Perhaps this is what I should do with my time, take up archaeology or some such, as I do seem to have a liking for the ancient world. I like the unknown connectivity. I remember some second-rate celeb on a TV show about ancestry was found to be related to royalty, and then it transpired that we were probably all cousins oft-removed to the great and the good of the past. So maybe there's a genetic link somewhere from the bloke who carved that column all those years back and me. I mean, equally maybe there isn't, but it makes you think. Or perhaps it just makes me think ...

I wonder too whether they had the time, intellect or inclination for introspection, the like of which frankly I am currently experiencing virtually ad nauseam. Did some Roman soldier notice a local girl, catch her eye and then walk away without doing anything about it? Did he spend twenty years of his life drinking wine to cover his fear? Then later, had he settled as a veteran, farming some harsh land in the Vale of York with this city visible from his front door? Did he think of that girl and wonder if his life would have been significantly different if only he'd spoken with her?

Probably not, I conclude, because chances are he wasn't a massive dickhead.

Time for a drink I think. To maintain the historical theme of the day I go to the Roman Baths – imaginatively named thus because the pub is built over Roman Baths. There's a basement with a small museum, but frankly I want alcohol more than I want any further ancient culture right now.

I buy a pint of local bitter and sit on my own. I fancy a cigarette, but I have vowed to myself and to Ailsa that I'd try to stop; and at my age tempting the gods to give me lung cancer or a stroke is probably not the best possible plan. So, and I say this with a slightly sinking heart, hoping Dear Friend that you'll indulge me just a wee bit more, back to the self-analysis.

Why do I feel the constant need to revisit where I came from? Does it help me know where I am now? Or is it indeed just pure self-indulgence: a wankfest sponsored by the Handy Andie organisation? I'm pretty sure it's the latter. I don't think our parents went in for this stuff, I can't imagine my serious, grown-up dad doing so anyway. They were just too busy bringing up kids, providing for the family and being responsible and adult – all those things that my baby-boomer post-hippy supposedly liberal generation, with our mortgages, affairs and divorces, tattoos and body piercings, trips to fucking find ourselves in Thailand and Glastonbury – are just too fucking busy to actually be arsed to attempt.

The focus used to be, I believe, on successful and straightforward transitioning from teenager into adulthood. Get there, get a job, work hard, meet a partner, settle down, buy a house, have kids, save for a new Humber and a colour telly – and maybe, just maybe, go abroad a couple of times. That was my mum and dad's life and that was life pretty much for most of their contemporaries. Stay together, be strong and bring your kids up the same way. Maybe the post-war difference was for my generation, the expectation that in the seventies if you had half a brain you'd go to university, but that was still fine. At twenty-one you'd leave, go out into the big, bad world and fend for yourself – leaving your mum and dad satisfied happy at the job they'd done and heading exhausted towards retirement.

Well that the was the middle-class world I grew up in at least, and it's not done me much harm except for two formerly – now hopefully reformed – dysfunctional children and an ex-wife who occasionally I want to shag and an ongoing love affair with strong liquor. Oh, and a constant nagging doubt that actually perhaps I am indeed the most self-indulgent, least well-balanced human being on God's earth. If the BBC ran a Mental Onanist of the Year competition, I'm pretty sure I'd be crowned perpetual champion.

The beer's good and I buy another. The pub's half-full of tourists who come for a drink after gawping at the baths and some locals gawping at the tourists.

I like the North of England again, I decide, switching to less dense introspection. I was forcibly shipped here like some convict guilty of nicking a farthing when I was a kid and so I resented it deeply – but actually there's a humility to the place and the people. It very much is a different country, to the leafy, pretentious, self-serving dosh-obsessed South East. Sure some of the shops I've walked past in this city are full of the same designer wank you'd get on

Guildford High Street and mysteriously Harvey Nicks opened in Leeds a few years back – but they seem to be the exceptions, catering for the demands of the minority of locals who are moneyed; students from wealthy backgrounds; and the southern owners of second homes in the Dales. The Real North, I muse, is a little more authentic, the topography is less parcelled and chocolate boxy than down South and the people more genuine and authentic. I could live in the North, once more, I conclude, in a cottage on the edge of a windswept moor, on my own. Perhaps that's it, that's the answer. I should decamp up here and buy a place in the land of my maternal grandfather near Pickering. I could wear an old tweed jacket and take on the curmudgeonly characteristics of say Geoff Boycott (without the bigotry and misogyny, though) and drive a beat-up, but terribly functional, Land Rover through fords in lambing season.

And that's the difference. For once, anything is possible for me. Apart from having responsibilities to ensure my kids don't turn into druggies (or work in reinsurance), I can do what the fuck I like when I like it, because, for the first time ever, I have money. I don't have to worry about paying the bills, I have the dosh. I could go and live anywhere at any time and it might just be in Yorkshire.

'You taking oop whole fuckin' table,' an old bloke sitting down opposite me states or possible asks. It's a little difficult to tell which from his accent and facial expression (which is one frankly of contempt). I realise he's with three mates and I'm hogging two seats. 'I'm sorry. Let me move ...' I begin to say when the old charmer continues, 'Only me and me friends always sit here, as it's our fookin' table.' He's not being aggressive as such, I realise, because he's too old to attempt to thump even me, but I know that he truly would like to punch me in my seemingly posh gob, if only he had the strength.

'Why don't I move then?' I say reasonably, looking at my remaining half pint.

'Good idea,' he says.

'Why don't I move when I'm good and ready you ridiculous old fucker?' I say looking him in the eye. 'You can take your gritty Boycott Yorkshire shit and stick it up your gritty Yorkshire arse. OK?'

He looks a little dumbfounded. I'm a little dumfounded too but that image of the girl from thirty-odd years ago, sniggering at my expense is in the forefront of my mind. I'm fucking fifty something and no one, least of all this old bastard, is going to treat me like shit again.

He looks at his friends who are all trying to disappear. 'There's no need to take that tone lad,' he says. 'And,' here he looks around the pub, 'thou should mind your language lad. There are ladies present you foul-mouthed cunt.'

Perhaps I won't move to Yorkshire after all.

I have another pint just to spite the bastards. They sit in sullen silence while I drink slowly. The barmaid, a cheery Yorkshire lass who's possibly spend too much time and money in the local chip shop or pie factory, comes over and say to the old sod, 'You bothering this gent Joe?'

I jump in and say, before the old bastard can reply, 'Landlady, Joe and his friends are an absolute delight regaling me as they are with such wit and wonderful Yorkshire repartee. What a pleasure it has been to spend time with such wonderful local characters, and I thank you for it.' She walks off shaking her head in bewilderment and smiling.

'Right gents,' I say breezily, standing up. 'Who'd like a drink?' to which old Joe says 'Don't mind if I do. Bitter would be nice.'

I reply, 'You know where the bar is you old Yorkshire cunt. Get it yourself,' and walk out of the pub feeling a ghost has disappeared.

I eat at a wee French place on my own. A good meal, half the price of a London equivalent. I order a bottle of wine and the waitress queries 'A whole bottle sir?' as I am obviously on my own here. Another glass of house red with the cheese, a coffee and a brandy and I'm sure the entire waiting staff have me down as an alcoholic. But I am now fit for my bed.

I have an uneventful walk back to the hotel and feel surprisingly happy, free and content.

17. Further on Up the Road

I breakfast well, indulging in the full English fry-up: a fabulous invention and one that separates the English from all other nations of the world, at least in terms of giving the population chronic heart problems.

I'm on the road by 9.30. I'm in Northumberland proper, Corbridge to be precise, at 11.45. I visit the museum and the fort but the splendour of yesterday's visit has rather sated me of things historic. I drive on to Housesteads on Hadrian's Wall itself.

I'm killing time, but I do love this part of the world. It's bleak and you get a real sense of space and sky. What would some poor bastard centurion from Gaul or Assyria or somewhere else in the Roman Empire, make of a posting here, where it's usually cold, normally raining, and full of people with strange accents? I park the car, pay the entrance fee and walk to the fort.

All that's left are stone outlines of the significant buildings that have been excavated. What's more impressive is the Wall that strikes out on either side of the fort clinging to the horizon. Oh God I think, perhaps I could live in a farmhouse and tend sheep on this land and wear a tweed jacket and drive an old functioning Land Rover ... Dear Reader you'll be pleased to hear that I stop these nonsensical musing and give myself a darn good talking to. Nope, this is a great place to visit – perhaps even take a holiday – but it's not truly, under any circumstance a place I could live in. If I was so disliked by the relatively soft southern (compared to this place) Joe in gentle York, I muse, what would his wild rugged Northumberland equivalent make of me? It's probably a bye-law that locals have to stick a shovel up the arse of all rich Southerners and leave them in a peat bog. And I would not protest against that outcome.

OK, I am not certain there are peat bogs in these parts. I'm just guessing. But you take my point? These are wild mysterious parts. I reckon the temple of Mithras just down the road is probably still being used as a regular place of worship.

It's time to go to Edinburgh.

Up through the border country past the Kielder Forest and through the National Park I drive. And it's great driving country especially in my nifty wee sports car. Perhaps I'll keep it after all. I'm getting slightly adventurous in it, putting my foot down to accelerate and overtake at speed. Money well spent, I conclude as I open the roof and slice through the wilderness.

As I hit the quaintness of the Scottish borders and their abbeys and tourist wool shops, my phone rings.

It's witchcraft I conclude as the sound system in the car has picked the call up. I pull over, and rather proudly press a button and I am connected to my caller. What will they think of next ...?

It is Henry, my fuckwitted and faux-cockney financial adviser.

'Alright Jamie?' he asks.

'Yes Henry, I'm splendid,' I reply.

Before I can ask after him he blurts out 'We've lost some money mate.'

I ask him how? And how much? I feel a little sick.

He explains that what with the subprime collapse my investment portfolio had lost fifteen per cent overnight.

'Fuck,' I say insightfully, like a dye-in-the-wool Gnome of Zurich.

'Fuck,' he agrees.

'Is the rest of my money safe?' I ask him.

'I've moved it around' he said. 'That's why I've been trying to get hold of you. To de-risk. I've piled you into Government Bonds and straight into a couple of banks that ain't gonna go tits up. If they do, the world will go tits up with them. Honestly Jamie, because you were so straight in your investments, you've dodged a bullet, mate'.

'I'm fifteen per cent worse off than I was though Henry. That's a lot of money'.

'Mate, some of my clients have lost their shirts.'

We chat some more but my heart is not in it. What's the point? It's not his fault the global financial system is in free fall. I decide to be sanguine about it. After all, I did kind of win the lottery. What Lady Luck gives, she can take away. I end the conversation by saying. 'Invest the rest of it wisely, make up the loss over time, buy me a decent lunch and I'll forgive you.'

I sit there for a couple of minutes. What I've just lost would take a nurse over thirty years to earn which is absurd and obscene in itself. But the truth is, I've never felt the money belonged to me anyway. I kind of won it in a corporate sweepstake.

I drive off on the countdown to Edinburgh: through Peebles towards Penicuik, thinking. I should feel rage but who against? Certainly not Henry as, despite his sometime bloated sense of self, he isn't solely responsible for the global financial markets. Nope, the blame sits with unbridled fucking capitalism and the entire world brown-nosing the bankers.

By the time I hit the Edinburgh ring road, with its miles of stationery traffic, I am reconciled to my loss. I've still enough money for the rest of my life and I can make sure the kids have a good financial start to their adulthood without going all Patty Hearst on me. It feels like a warning shot that, no matter how good life might become, you just might still get a sharp implement shoved up your backside, without either lubrication or indeed your consent, if the gods so deem it. Shit happens and a lot worse shit happens to people than what has just hit me.

I'm alive. David isn't.

With that thought I remember Ailsa. I'd forgotten to call her, despite Helen's message. Bugger. Self-obsessed as usual. I make the call and, of course, it goes to voicemail. I tell her how much I enjoyed our lunch, that I want to do it again soon perhaps with Nick next time, and I'd call her when I was home.

Duty done. Terrible father.

And that brings me back to my current predicament as the ring road ends at the Maybury roundabout and I turn toward the city, then cut up towards Barnton and Cramond. I start to wonder what I am letting myself in for. I am about to knock on the door of a grieving widow and her bereft children and talk about a guy I knew forty years ago, but who I had seen precisely fifteen times subsequently. I am staying at their house and eating their food and drinking their drink.

On that point I stop at the Barnton Co-op and avail myself of a half-decent bottle of malt and whatever passes for fine wine in that establishment. I suspect genteel Edinburgh folk in Cramond are not quite ready for my binge drinking abilities so some subterfuge may be needed.

The area is as I remember it – large stone houses, the wee row of shops, the Royal Burgess Golfing Society with its mock Tudor façade which is where drinks and a buffet are to take place after the funeral. The car park is full of financiers' expensive motors. A lot of those will probably be going back to the dealerships given the financial collapse, I think with some relish, which is rather ill-spirited of me, I recognise.

When we were kids, we used to cycle past David's family home and be in awe of it. It had two wonderful round towers facing the road, and a stream at the bottom of the garden, which in those days we could paddle in. We talked then of living in that house one day. Well, David had achieved that. Now there's a high wall with steel spikes on top to keep out intruders, and mature trees blocking out much of the natural light. There's a main gate which I drive up to cautiously. Remarkably it opens as I approach it. Someone must have seen the car and recognised the English number plates.

I pull up beside a Porsche 4x4 and a huge Mercedes and get out of my car. As I approach the front door it opens and there stands Kathlyn.

Wow. Kathlyn. She'd always been a good-looking woman. The last time I'd seen her had been at their wedding, which must have been some twenty-five years ago. She'd been stunning then. She looks stunning now.

But she's matured and matured well. Dark hair, I don't think dyed, is swept back off a face that is lightly tanned, fine cheek bones, lips with just enough lipstick to be the correct side of saucy. She's dressed in a black dress that accentuates a fine figure. She looks tired and drawn, but I guess that's understandable as her husband, the father of her children and my oldest friend, is lying in a pine (well, probably ancient oak) box at a funeral directors a couple of miles away.

OK she's had the money to look after herself properly, but she hasn't that haunted unnatural look of the woman who's been under the surgeons' knife or spends hours at the beauticians. She's just a great-looking woman and one to whom age has been kind.

'Jamie,' she says holding out her hand which I take, and then move forward to kiss her cheek. 'Kathlyn,' I say 'I am so, so sorry,' and I mean it. As we briefly cling to each other, I feel human again. (And no there are no trouserly stirrings, how can you even think such a thing? What do you take me for?) I'm holding my oldest friend's recently widowed wife, I am comforting her. And I feel deeply sad, at last, for her loss and indeed mine.

' I am so, so sorry,' I say again, my eyes tearing up as I do. 'David was such a lovely man. This is all so ... unfair.'

She sniffs near my ear in a way that such a perfectly-poised woman probably shouldn't sniff, but at least it indicates she's human. We untangle ourselves and I get my bag from the car.

'Come in,' she says. 'Meet the kids'.

We go up the front steps past two large stone lions, through a massive shining black front door and into the hall. Everything about the place smacks of a baronial pile in the stewardship of the National Trust. Everywhere antique furniture, pictures and paintings. An impressive entrance to the house, but not a warm, friendly one.

She takes me into a TV room off the hall and there are two kids comatose in front of *The Simpsons*. 'Calum, and Kirsty!' she says to attract their attention from the TV. They turn to look up at me. The boy is about seventeen and is the spitting image of David at that age, and the girl, a couple of years younger, I guess, will grow into her mother. 'This is Jamie,' she says, 'a very old friend of your daddy's. Jamie, this is Kirsty and Calum.' No response. 'He'll be here until Daddy's funeral.' A languid arm goes up from the Calum, I am not certain whether of dismissal or greeting.

'Don't worry,' I whisper to Kathlyn. 'It's difficult at this age. Mine barely talk to me and I'm still alive,' I say and then kind of regret the insensitivity of the remark. She smiles. 'Tea? Coffee?' she asks as she guides me towards an open plan kitchen.

'A cup of tea would be lovely,' I say, thinking that a large glass of alcohol would be even lovelier still – but I won't get it in this house at this time. But as if she can read my mind she says, 'Unless you'd like a proper drink? I think under the circumstances we probably both deserve one. A G&T perhaps? Or a glass of wine?' I plump for wine.

'Oh, and I brought these,' I say, proffering the Co-op's finest.

'That's thoughtful,' she says with a smile. 'Bring them here,' and she opens one of the doors off the kitchen to reveal a sunken wine cellar.

'I don't think these are worthy of a place down there,' I say, smiling. 'They'll probably ruin the good stuff. Why don't I just unscrew this one?' – screw-top wine, here? Fuck she must think me an impoverished uncultured buffoon.

Again she smiles, as she reaches for two wine glasses. In the spacious kitchen, all teak and stainless steel and a range that looks like it could cater for all the inhabitants of Cramond and its environs – she looks for all the world like a suburban host kicking off a dinner party, not a damned fine-looking recently-widowed top Edinburgh lawyer. Which incidentally she is.

I take a slug of the passably good Norwegian Merlot or whatever I grabbed in a mild panic at the Co-op. 'Cheers, Jamie,' she says and she takes a more refined sip. She's far too polite to grimace. Polish this one off, I think and then perhaps I'll get access to David's well-stocked cellar. Bet he won't even notice ...

I'm brought up short by the realisation that of course the poor bastard won't notice as he is dead. He will never step back through that front door again to claim his Château Lafite, at least not in human form. Again that wave of sadness, and something approximating to self-hatred, as I realise the insensitivity of my thinking. It strikes me that, David's death will affect me the next couple of days, but I will move on from this temporary grief. I'll probably think about him occasionally, but my world will keep turning, I'll get over it. These people understandably will find it much more difficult. Everyday they spend in this house there'll be pang of someone, something, missing. When the kids are older and have moved on, when the house has been sold on and is occupied by some other captain of industry and his family, Calum and Kirsty will return periodically, drive past the huge gates and remember that it was here that they last saw their father alive.

I'm hopelessly sentimental for the past (I'm telling you nothing you don't already know) and I obsess over and recollect the smallest detail of my own frankly tepid upbringing. How the fuck might I have coped with something like this happening to me at such a tender age?

We move to a massive living room. Large bay windows open out to a well-cared-for rose garden and a stone-clad patio. The room itself is oak-panelled with a large fireplace blocked during what allegedly passes for summer in Edinburgh by a large vase of dried reeds and thistles. There are oil paintings on the wall: Victorian scenes of Scottish Highlands, small smoke-emitting crofts and happy highlanders returning from their day's work – presumably unaware that a bunch of lowland bastards (and no, not just the English by the way) are hiding over the next hill waiting to clear them from their lands and replace them with sheep.

There are a couple of expensive-looking painting of horses racing, and some scenes of early golf. There are Victorian bronzes on dark-wood cabinets and huge rustic-looking vases filled with dried flowers. Everything looks very expensive indeed, but none of it is to my taste. As I sit down on a huge leather banquette, I'm reminded of an upmarket golf club or a country hotel in the Borders. It's just – what's the word I'm looking for? – soulless, a kind of temple to Sir Walter Scott's (the father of the tartan biscuit tin, arguably and by the way) idea of Scottishness.

Indeed there are leather-bound books in floor-to-ceiling shelves on either side of the fireplace and I can see from this that a lot of Sir Walter features. I'm not knocking Scott as a writer – the first truly global author brand – but because of him people whose Scottish heritage links back to their grandad once being on a bus in Glasgow, now get married in Guildford in Moss Bros kilts and ghillie brogues and skean dhu poking out the top of their sock.

She sees me looking. 'This was David's room bless him,' she says. 'He loved his pictures of Scotland. He collected it all himself – going into those ridiculously expensive antique shops on Queen Street and the Royal Mile – looking for things to help recreate his view of the Scottish pastoral. He was probably the only customer they had from outside North America. He was ... quite insecure was our David.'

Surprisingly she takes a cigarette out and offers one to me. I decline with a shake of the head, Ailsa's voice ringing. She lights it, draws on and exhales a long plume of smoke into the sunlit room. She's a woman that obviously likes to smoke.

'OK I'd never have smoked in here when David was alive,' she says. 'Barely smoked anyway, only at times of stress and never in the house. He hated me smoking.' She took another pull and said 'But it's not me that's dead from a massive heart attack now is it?' And she smiles somewhat bitterly.

'Insecure?' I say, trying to ignore her casual callousness and needing to prompt her to expand upon this possible weakness in my old friend.

'Oh Christ, yes. Riddled with insecurities.' A swig of wine and she says, 'Of course all this ... shit, ' and here she dismissively points around the room and its contents. 'It's all terribly tasteless Victorian expensive tat. He bought it just to show people that he – from a fairly humble background – had arrived. He was a success and here,' again, a lofty wave of her hand encompassing the room, the baronial house and the garden, 'was the proof. I shall sell it all at auction unless it goes with the house.' I glance up at her in surprise. 'Yes, as soon as the funeral's over this place is on the market. New start for all of us.' A drag on the fag.

I feel sad for David. His parents had been very ordinary and he'd grown up (as I had arguably ...) on a bog standard 1960's middle-class estate of newly built houses. Perhaps that remained in his DNA and his proud collecting of all things relating to Scottish tins of shortbread, was trying to somehow counteract what he felt inside. Ordinary. Even perhaps with Kathlyn, whose parents were rather less ordinary: one a professor at the university, the other partner in one of Edinburgh's oldest legal practices, and who had been brought up in a massive detached house in Morningside – perhaps he'd always felt ordinary in comparison to her. And he was overcompensating through kitsch.

I can honestly say, I had never recognised even the vaguest potential for David to feel ordinary.

She finishes her glass of wine and helps herself to another. I get up and do the same as she seems distracted by her thoughts and she's no intention obviously of trying to be the perfect hostess.

She goes on, 'Of course you know that dear, sweet, hardworking simple David did have his dark side? Of course you do, Jamie,' she checks herself, 'he confided in you a few years ago, I believe?' She fixes me with a stare.

OK, Jamie so be careful here, I tell myself. I *think* I know what she's referring to: his falling off the marital straight and narrow and into the slender and presumably tender arms of the fair Alison. Another reason I had to feel inferior to him as she really was a gorgeous woman. Kathlyn finding out had not gone well for him, I remember. David had told me of the fallout – how she'd slung him out initially, then taken him back in (he thought out of shame in front of their particularly well-heeled professional friends), to a purgatorial existence of sleeping on a sofa for months on end – which was particularly ironic as the house probably had about ten perfectly pleasant and functional bedrooms, where they could have avoided each other for months. And then latterly, when they returned to a semblance of what passed for marital normality (whatever precisely the fuck that looks like), it was obvious she'd never quite forgiven him fully. Why should she? I thought. Hell, wrath, scorned women and all that sprung to mind.

But perhaps there had been others he'd never told me about. Or even worse, perhaps he'd been flaunting his middle-aged but still sickeningly toned body around the lorry parks of Scotland (given you'd be hard pushed to find a functioning fishing fleet nowadays). 'Dark side' does sound a little more interesting than, frankly, a workplace bunk-up. But the simple fact is, I don't know what I'm supposed to know about their relationship, and there's a danger here that I dig a massive hole and fall in head first.

Sensibly stalling and gathering my thoughts, I say, 'Do you know what? I think I will join you in that cigarette after all.' OK, sorry, Ailsa, but extenuating circumstances have never been more extenuating than right now.

We make a bit of a fuss lighting the ciggy and arranging the ashtray so that we've both got easy access and that buys me a little time.

She's looking at me. She know I'm deliberately hesitating. She wants, she needs, a reaction, from me. Here goes ... 'Oh Kathlyn I wouldn't call it a dark side as such, you know. He was hardly Alistair Crowley' (an unwise reference perhaps, I realise, given the power of the Kirk in these social circles, but hey, when did sensitivity ever get in the way of the opportunity for a poor, cheap joke *chez moi*?). I stagger on. 'Fundamentally he was a good man, a man who loved you and the kids and was loyal and caring. That's the David I knew.' Slurp. Pulse racing.

'Loyal?' she practically spits out. 'Loyal when he was fucking his PA?.' And there's something about the word 'fucking' when it's used by very posh folk, regardless of regional accent, that's strangely enticing. 'Oh, come on,' she continues 'please Jamie, spare me the *fucking* platitudes.'

What is it about me? I mean, should I refer myself to some pervert register? I'm on the cusp of an emotional exchange with my old mate's recent widow, I am steeling myself to both defend his honour and try to reconcile this woman to her dead husband's long virtuous life, marred only by the teensiest of slips (arguably understandable in my not so very humble opinion) with the aforementioned Alison, and two uses of the F-word in her Morningside accent I'm experiencing nascent trouserly stirrings (or NTS as I believe the condition may be known in pervert circles.) I mean – shallow or what?

'Oh Kathlyn,' I say taking a slug of wine and a drag on the fag to buy me some more time. 'You know that was an aberration, that wasn't the real David. The real David was loyal and loving and caring. He just slipped. It happens, you know,' I say, nodding sagely as if it's happened to me many, many times with gorgeous women half my age. 'He worked hard,' I continued, in what I consider to be a learned and understanding voice, which mercifully seems to be quelling the previously mentioned NTS. 'He wanted to provide for you and the kids and looking at all this,' I wave in mock admiration of our Walker Shortbread Tin surroundings, 'this was his way of trying to do that. He just slipped. It happens when people are under pressure.'

She looks straight at me. She has a hard face in this light, a combination of drink and grief and tiredness. I feel for her. David was a prick for ruining what he'd worked so hard for. She sobs a little. 'Well it shouldn't have happened,' she says sadly. 'It's such a fucking ... cliché. The wee wife sat at home whilst the hubby's out earning the crusts and shagging the milkmaids. Jamie, it's rubbish in this day and age. Life's moved on from that surely. He was a better man that that. I mean, don't you think I've had my fair few opportunities for extra marital flings?'

'I'm sure you have,' I say waiting, for more.

She shifts slightly uncomfortably in her chair, her eyes looking out through the patio doors into the expanse of their large garden. She seems lost. Perhaps, I speculate , she's recalling the frisson of a post-cocktail flirt at some lawyer's conference twenty years ago. And then I realise there's something else. I think, based on precisely no evidence, whatsoever, that she broke a marital vow or two, way before David's adventure. Why has that even sprung to my mind? Well she's protesting too much. Yes, she's hurt and angry but most of all, there's something disappointed about her. David had the courage to go from a one nighter to a fully-fledged and oft spunk-fest of an affair and she regrets she hadn't done the same.

Dear Reader, I understand your scepticism. I've not turned into Mystic Meg , but I just know that this affronted, hurt woman is suffering from guilt herself and that's what really hurts her. I'm certain, but it's not a certainty I can express in any way to her.

'It's all just so clichéd and tawdry and so fucking, *fucking* cheap and unfair.' Oh that word again from this twin set and pearls woman.

'Look, you have to park this sometime, Kathlyn, you really do. He was a good man, a very good man, but he was flawed ultimately like every one of us is. No, actually', I contradict myself, 'he was less flawed than most of the rest of us.'

'I admire your loyalty, Jamie,' she says.

'I'm only speaking as I find,' I reply, sagely I feel, draining the glass, and finishing the cigarette.

'More?' she asks. I take another ciggy, drain the remains of my bottle in to my glass and wonder what the evening has in store.

18. Sweet Dreams (Are Made of This)

We have a sombre meal, cooked quickly and quite effectively by Kathlyn. The kids are polite and in the main silent. I do my best to draw something out of them. Calum has just turned seventeen and goes to The Academy (obviously) and likes languages and maths. Wants to go into the bank like his father. I make a feeble joke asking him why he doesn't want to do something worthwhile. You can feel the lead poison in the room from the descending balloon as I do so. Yes, he plays golf and rugby, 'But not half as well as Dad,'. He tells me proudly that his dad had a handicap of three (he's a bit more handicapped than that now I think, then hate myself immediately) and he got a B cap for Scotland Under 18s before a serious injury stopped him playing at a senior level.

The poor lad. His father's death has frozen things in time for him, I think. He's always going to be saddled with comparisons with no chance to excel and be congratulated by his father. Usually happens – how do the children of very successful men compete with their all-conquering fathers? In most cases they can't – they're a disappointment or a challenge. No wonder so many go into drugs or drink and don't even try for success. I truly hope this boy is not the same.

For an Edinburgh Academy pupil, he's actually a nice kid.

The girl, I am told, has just turned sixteen, but looks a lot older. It's patently obvious she doesn't want to be here and understandably doesn't want me here either. This whole death thing – she doesn't know what's expected of her, she doesn't know what to do or how to behave, because she's not quite confident enough to just do as she feels. There's a lot of pent-up anger here. And I remember David telling me that he worried about her the most; that he thought she could be vulnerable. Looking at her here, I think she's storing up big issues for a possibly very rebellious adolescence .

The children of wealth tend to be neglected by their parents who are obsessed either with making or spending money. In this family's case, they're further screwed up from the norm by the premature death of David. Thankfully, I reflect, my (recently dwindled) money has only come to me recently and my offspring were well screwed-up previously under relative poverty. I want to say wise things to these kids, to give them some perspective, but there's nothing I can say that will ease their sense of loss.

The meal is over, the kids disappear and I help clear up. Kathryn's been quite silent during dinner as if she doesn't quite know what to say to her own children. She's drunk quite heavily too, as have I, but I suspect I have had rather more experience of this than she.

'Let's have a wee nightcap,' she says with a slight slur while proffering a bottle of aged malt. I pour a decent measure for her, an obscenely indecent measure for myself, and we do the decent Scottish thing of adding a smidgeon of water. We go outside into the relative warmth of a late spring Edinburgh evening. She offers me a cigarette and I take one without comment. She lights it and then hers and exhales into the night.

'Thanks,' she says after a reflective pause. 'Thanks for earlier. You're right. He was one of the good guys. It's just that now he's not here to punish, I'm just left with an anger that has nowhere to go. It just ...' she starts to sob, 'disappears into emptiness.'

And the sobbing becomes stronger and suddenly I'm holding her, juggling whisky glass and cigarette in one hand, trying not to lose either or combine the two and set us both on fire like some suburban Buddhist monk tribute band.

She just shakes into my shoulders and we stay there for a few minutes lost but finding some comfort in close human contact.

And no, I didn't get trouserly stirrings Dear Reader. How dare you even think, let alone suggest, such a thing. Even pervy Jamie knows what's appropriate and when.

We stand there, saying nothing, the noise of traffic and planes descending into the airport nearly drowning out the birdsong. And I think what a strange world it is where this woman is leaning into me, a relative stranger, for comfort. We barely know each other,

'Let's go in Kathlyn,' I say gently, after about five minutes of her clinging to me, taking a pull on the cigarette (feeling a flash of guilt towards Ailsa as I do) and draining my glass. 'I need another drink.'

We go in, we both refill our glasses and she says quietly, 'Thanks for being there Jamie. I know we don't know each other, but ... I feel close to you. You're very ... comforting. Thank you.'

'No need to thank me,' I say. 'It's what I'm here for. These are strange, emotional times for you all. I can't imagine what you're going through, how you're keeping yourself going. And keeping the kids going, too. So if my role is to comfort, that's fine.'

Do you know what? I think I've got a bit of a talent for this homespun counselling. I think I'm rather good at it – indeed better at identifying and sorting out other people's problems than my own. I should consider a second career in it.

She looks straight at me. She's still beautiful but in the dimmed lights she looks – not unsurprisingly given recent circumstances – tired and old. 'But sorry, Jamie. What must you think of me? Sobbing all over you when we barely know each other. I just needed ... contact. So, sorry but thank you. You're a lovely man. David was right about you. You're a good friend.'

There's part of me that's a wee bit hurt. A lovely man who makes her feel comfortable. That's a bit boring – like being compared to fleecy carpet slippers or a mangy old cardigan. Those things are comforting, comfortable. And a 'lovely man'? Bit safe, bit boring, at least compared with my life of the last week or so. She could at least have alluded to a secret crush on me that she'd not been able to shake off since she last saw me, which was on her wedding day. How me holding her had conjured up long-forgotten feelings of passion. That would have bolstered the old ego ce soir, whereas this makes me feel a wee bit ... boring.

She sits and I force myself to stop this particular line of thought. I should take 'boring' –even if self-defined – as a positive. I've been useful. I'm doing something for David, even if the bastard isn't here to acknowledge it and thank me.

'Another?' she asks looking at my empty glass and I inexplicably reply, 'Is the Pope from Cowdenbeath?'

and she laughs insincerely. I think I've just gone from comforting to whatever folk from Morningside call a knobhead.

We swap memories. I tell her of David's impossible and improbable perfection in any sporting environment: his prowess at rugby, tennis, cricket, squash and football. If playing darts, pool and table footy would not have offended his sense of social status he'd have excelled at those, too, undoubtedly. How I used to try to kick the living crap out of him when the difference in our ages actually meant something and I was bigger and stronger than him. 'But the wee bastard, even when he was about eight years of age so, was fast and I couldn't get near him to kick him,' I tell her.

She laughs. 'Your Scottish accent returned there,' she says smiling and holding my gaze, perhaps a little too long. Uh oh, I think, be careful what you wish for, she's had an awful lot to drink and seems suddenly very relaxed, less prissy. Deflection tactics needed, I feel.

I plough on 'Then when he got his first at St. Andrew's and he joined the bank and was a regional director before he was thirty, I knew he was moving out of my league success-wise. Focused, driven. Oh and naturally smart and charming. All the things I wasn't. More reasons to hate the wee bastard.' I smile, as does she.

'But you've come good, Jamie. David told me. Some share options – you've done well for yourself, too. He was really pleased for you, I remember.' He must have heard something on the financial grapevine

'Carpetbagger,' I say. She looks at me puzzled. 'That's what I am, a carpetbagger, a chancer. Lucked out, big time. Might as well have won the lottery.'

'Rubbish,' she says. 'You were obviously smart. And charismatic. David always said so.'

'Truly, Kathlyn,' I say, staring at my drink, feeling pissed and tired. 'I just got very, very lucky.'

'You're very hard on yourself,' she observes. 'I mean first impressions of you are that you're confident, possibly a wee bit overconfident?'

I smile. 'I have been accused of that, it's true.'

'But you're full of insecurities, like everybody else. And you don't always try to hide them.'

'Half a bottle of very good Scotch does tend to help me with my self-honesty issues.' I realise here that the counsellor has just been a wee bit counselled.

There's silence, then she says 'I'd like you to say something at the funeral. If that's OK? I know it's what David would have wanted.'

'I'd be delighted,' I reply then correct myself. 'Honoured. Not delighted. Utterly the wrong word there. I'd be honoured.'

'It's a fairly formal affair. You know what the Kirk's like,' she says. 'Thanks for agreeing to do the reading. There are a couple of work colleagues saying things and the the minister knew him well so he'll do the main eulogy. After that, it's you. There's not many folk that can boast a friendship as long as yours.'

'It would be my honour,' I say raising my glass.

Shit, shit, shit, I think! I'd kind of forgotten that I was to participate.

There is one little fact that I have omitted to tell, you Dear Reader, and have not told this woman because she hasn't asked – but I hate public speaking. Hate it with a passion.

'What would you like me to read?' I ask, attempting nonchalance.

She gets up, slightly unsteadily I notice, opens a draw in a sideboard and takes out a piece of folded paper. As she passes it to me she says 'Ecclesiastes, you know the one. Time for living. That one. Maybe a bit of a cliché but ... David read it at his father's funeral. Seems appropriate.'

'It's a wonderful piece,' I say. 'I shall try to do it justice. I promise.'

'Thank you,' she says. 'I shall go to bed now. Big day tomorrow.'

'Me too,' I say. 'I'm done in.'

We leave together, and go up the stairs. The master bedroom is at the far end of the football-pitch-sized hall, mine the opposite end. She stops. She kisses me on the cheek and says, 'Thank you. You're a true friend,' and squeezes my hand.

'Good night, Kathlyn,' I respond. 'Sweet dreams.'

Sweet dreams? Sweet dreams, you fucking idiot? You've just said 'sweet dreams' to a widow who is attending her recently prematurely-dead husband's funeral tomorrow. You master of compassion.

I walk nonchalantly to my room cursing myself, hoping she's too pissed to remember the inappropriateness of my inane response.

Aha I think there is a God in heaven as I remember the sneaked bottle of Scotch in my suitcase. A tumbler of that and I will indeed be ready for the sleep of the just.

19. Tombstone Blues

I wake up the next morning to the sounds of a household also waking up. Doors banging a few cross words between children and mother and I realise I've not experienced this myself for a couple of years. Strangely, I miss it.

Jesus, I think. I confess I've felt better. I've forgotten the downside of smoking. Lung disease and heart conditions aside, the fags don't half exacerbate a hangover.

My room, as you'd expect, is like something you'd experience at the Balmoral Hilton. Obviously it has an en suite bathroom so I use the lavatorial facilities, shave and shower in peace and dignity. I put on my black Hugo Boss suit. I look good I have to admit it, though my head feels like the inside of a Highlander's sporran after a weekend of excessive caber tossing.

I head downstairs towards the kitchen where the noise is coming from, and as I enter I am confronted by a blond woman in her early twenties. I do think I've died and joined David in some amongst the angels. She is truly stunning, Slavic cheeks, almond-blue eyes, blond hair swept back off her face, her body encased in a tight T-shirt and tight black denim jeans.

'You like ex?' she asks without ceremony and I gulp for air. The kids are already at the breakfast table. The blonde beauty looks at me contemptuously and then says to them 'He wants sex?'

They then look at me and I wonder what I have stumbled in to. Was David keeping this vision as a sex slave for friends and family? No wonder Kathryn was so reluctant to allow his return to the marital bed. Was there, after all, no end to this man's depravity?

'This is Jana,' says Calum patiently. 'Jana – Jamie, an old friend of my father,' he says this with a suaveness and confidence that belies his years. He will go places, this boy. She shakes my hand enthusiastically and smiles a smile that could melt a stone funeral tribute. Calum goes on 'She's asking if you want eggs.'

'Eggs? Oh yes please,' I say, with some relief. 'Eggs. Please.'

Sometimes I realise I can be such an arsehole.

I make small talk with the kids. They're still in dressing gowns and they look pale and worried, not unexpectedly. 'It'll be fine,' I say, soothingly. 'You'll do your dad proud.' The girl's eyes swell with tears.

Jana appears with a Scottish low-calorie breakfast – just one piece of fried bread. And black pudding, sausages, mushrooms, fried potato, beans, haggis and bacon. A feast for a king served by a vision.

'Where are you from Jana?' I ask.

'Poland,' she replies. 'Krakow.'

I stifle an admittedly pathetic snigger, Always makes me laugh, Krakow. Like Clitheroe. And let's not forget Cockermouth.

Sometimes I can't wait for my fourteenth birthday.

'I au pair,' she goes on, as I attack the breakfast. 'Look after kids. Love kids. Loved Mr David, too,' and now she starts to cry which starts the girl off.

Lucky Mr David, I think and hate myself for doing so.

She leaves, then returns, composed, with a pot of tea. 'You English. You want tea always.' It's not a question, it's very much a statement.

Kathlyn enters. She too is in her dressing gown. She looks older and tired without her make-up. Understandable. I decide not to mention it.

'I see you've met Jana,' she says with a faint smile. 'Isn't she something?'

I can only nod my agreement.

She sits down, declines food, taking only a black coffee and some water. I wonder if she's regretting our wee drinking session last night.

The funeral is to start at Cramond Kirk at 11 am. There's a service, then we decamp to the Golf Club for what the Scots call, I believe, a Funeral Tea. I'm very much hoping this is what the English call a Funeral Piss-Up.

The next hour or so I spend reading the paper while everyone else busies themselves with getting ready. At ten the doorbell goes and gradually over the next hour or so the house fills with sobbing, grieving relatives all offering comfort and hugs to Kathlyn and the kids. I feel awkward, an interloper. I decide I should take myself off.

'I need fresh air,' I say quietly to Kathlyn, and I decide to walk to the local shop. I realise I cannot get through this day without a plentiful supply of cigarettes.

It's a bright slightly crisp morning. It takes me ten or so minutes to reach the shop and by the time I've further enhanced BAT's profit with sixty of their finest sticks of poison and leave the shop, the sky is dark and it's raining. Oh the joys of an Edinburgh summer I think. I spent ten years here as a kid and in all that time I can barely remember summer. Winter, yes, with snow piled high at the side of the road, but summer, no. And in the few times I have been back it's always the same. This fabulous gracious noble city with its culture and history has a *Blade Runner* climate without the warmth.

I get back to the house, the Boss style now a bit damp. Jana greets me offering coffee. She's now wearing a short, black, tight dress that accentuates her charms wonderfully and I wonder if she'd understand the English word 'Elope'.

There's a British efficiency to death. 10.30 and a fleet of black cars appears on the gravel drive. The hearse is there with a flower-encased coffin. A team of funerary flunkies step out and guide people into the limo hierarchically, close family in the first, distant relatives and friends in the other three cars. I've already decided to make my own way there. I walk to the car and Jana suddenly appears.

'Take me, please,' she says.

'We may just about have time before the funeral – I'm willing if you are, ' is the response that springs to mind but which, mercifully, I resist saying.

'Sure,' I say nonchalantly, and in a gentlemanly manner (is that sexist, by the way?) I open the passenger door and say 'hop in.' I resist looking at her fabulousness as she does so.

'Nice car,' she says patting the upholstery and donning a pair of designer sun glasses.

'Thanks,' I reply wittily and we head off in front of the funeral cortege to the Kirk.

I am a cliché, I realise. Middle-aged bloke, expensive sports car, blond half my age. What must I look like?

I turn left and head down the road I used to know so well towards the Kirk and the sea.

The Kirk is as I remember it when I was dragged there reluctantly on Sundays as a kid – only today, on this damp Wednesday morning, half of Lowland Scotland seems to have turned out. Taxis are pulling up, people are congregating on the street – there are literally hundreds of people and a queue of traffic heading to the car park. A few heads turn to look at my inappropriate sports car and the greying fattish bloke driving it with the gorgeous blond beside him. Even in this sombre occasion you can tell they disapprove.

We park. 'I'd like to take a walk if that's OK? Just to gather my thoughts,' I say.

Cramond Village always was genteel, sandstone villas towards the top part, and white fishermen's and mill workers' cottages towards the bottom near where the River Almond flows into the Firth of Forth. It's obviously still a 'wee gem' unknown to the tourists, as there are no shops just the pub, a museum and a café.

I realise Jana is walking beside me. To break the silence I say 'I used to come here as a kid. Long time ago.'

'Oh,' she replies, disinterested. Note to self, she really is not here to listen to the memories of a middle-aged bloke. It's cold and wet so we head back up the slope towards the Kirk.

I notice a round tower at the back of the car park, fifty feet or so tall, and memories appear from nowhere. When we were kids it was derelict and we imagined it to be haunted. We'd probably watched too many episodes of *Scooby-Doo,* but it genuinely used to scare us.

And then the memories do flood in, as memories can – a video clip montage of four or five summers of my youth – vision along with smells and sounds – and I am on my bike, a red, gearless racer, and I'm leading a bunch of guys, including David, from my street along the banks of the Almond. Someone – not me – has a transistor radio hanging from the handlebars of their Chopper bike, and I recall the crackled sound of Mungo Gerry's 'In the Summertime'. We fairly flew along that river bank feeling tough and hard and free, as walkers shouted at us to dismount as travelling on two wheels at that speed was obviously dangerous. I remember the mild roar of the river, the smell of damp foliage, the sun breaking through the trees, the wheels of my bike splattering the back of my shorts with the mud churned up by recent rain, and I recall a feeling of exhilaration and delight.

All that in the blink of an eye. I realise that the thirteen-year-old me – awkward, nervous, scared of what people thought of me, and whether they liked me – was, in that recollected moment of a summer long ago, truly happy, happier than the adult me has probably ever been.

Where has the time gone?

As we walk to the Kirk I think of David: ridiculously talented, clever and good-looking David. That's probably quite appropriate as I'm about to attend his funeral, I recognise. David – with the career and the wife and the well-educated kids and the house to die for, and the love and respect of his community and his peers – and I think, even David managed to fuck it up. Even David with his more than fair share of natural resources managed to screw up. Yes, Dear Reader, I confess that that realisation does bring me some comfort, even at this time as we're about to say goodbye to his mortal remains.

What sort of a sick fuck am I, I think, that even now at this point I have to score points against a dead man who was my friend? Thank God he didn't die suspiciously or else motive-wise I'd be in the frame.

We're a wee bit early and I am determined to be at the back of the church so I hang back. 'Jana, let me show you something,' I say and her beautiful Slavic features and almond eyes look into my face with absolute innocence.

We head away from the gaggle of people and we walk towards the grassed area at the back of the Kirk. 'This was a Roman fort,' I say, 'it defended the empire against the barbarous north.' Again, this is important to me as I remember walking here as a kid, trying to imagine what a posting here two thousand years ago must have been like with the virtually constant haar enveloping all. The main buildings are marked out on the ground by masonry, with explanatory plaques beside each.

'No fort here,' she says. 'Just little stones. Thought Romans built big buildings. Walls and coliseum? This bit shit,' she says looking at the flat grass.

I can't be arsed explaining. The youth of today, whether Slavic or British, don't really do imagination. A Roman fort needs to be rebuild in its entirety and offer the visitor the opportunity to slaughter barbarians – probably through computer simulations – to be of interest. So, I take out my packet of cigarettes, offer her one, She accepts unhesitatingly and we both smoke, me pensively, she distractedly.

It is, I sense, time to join the throng and we do so as the Kirk doors are opened. I look at the mourners as a few stub out their cigarettes and switch off their mobiles, many with a last-ditch look at their emails before radio silence ensues. In the main it's a collection of upper-middle-class, middle-aged men, some accompanied by wives or girlfriends. They look wealthy. Very few are slim – there's at best a jowliness to them, at worst a borderline obesity – all encased in obviously expensive suits and highly-polished handmade shoes. They murmur to each other as they shuffle in. They're men of wealth and of importance and they know it and here, even at the funeral of one of theirs, there's business to be done, hands to be shaken and gossip to be exchanged.

I watch them pass as I stand there with the beautiful Pole. It's a steady flow of privilege and I guess I'm part of that: although I'd argue that I've arrived at my wealth through different, more noble means. I haven't just been bailed out to the tune of several billion quid by HMG for a start. But now is probably not the time to consider a Marxist revolution.

And then she come through. I recognise her in a gaggle of other thirty-something women – Alison. She's trying to blend in; she's trying desperately not to be noticed, surrounded as she is by six or eight other people. But I see her. Her tear-stained eye catches mine and I nod. She ignores me. This is obviously some subterfuge of hers to say goodbye to the man she thought she probably loved. Suddenly this funeral – this stiff formal passionless event that will begin shortly with words from a religion that few people in the congregation truly believe in or live by (certainly not the bits about rich men, camels and needles, that's for sure) and will end with a friend's body being interred – looks as if it may be interesting.

But of course why should she recognise me? We only met the once a few years back and she was upset and probably pissed. So there's nothing to be read into the fact that she's ignored me. But I wonder mischievously, does Kathlyn know who Alison is? Is there going to be some sort of a catfight over the coffin that will shake this bunch of passionless bastards up a bit.

Oh Christ, I'm doing it again I realise. What sort of a friend, what sort of a human being wants the funeral of someone's husband, someone's father, ruined in such a way? Well not even me really, I guess. I can daydream, though, about scenes and arguments and the rending of garments – if only just to liven things up a bit and show some of these bastards to be just a little bit human

Jana and I enter the church and take our place towards the back in a packed pew. The Minister – an elderly, jowly, comfortably-off-looking guy, who from the look of him could have been plucked from the audience and given the job just moments before, so well does he blend into his audience – welcomes us and briefly.

Then it starts with a solitary piper, who plays a lament as he enters the Kirk. He's followed by four guys from the undertakers in black suits, carrying the coffin, draped in the flag of St Andrew, aloft. They march in time slowly to the front of the church. It is indeed moving theatre.

With the coffin safely laid out for all to see, the Minister then begins proceedings with the reading of Psalm 121 'I will lift up mine eyes unto the hills, from whence cometh my help'. Bit late for that I muse, for David at least. We then have a Gaelic hymn which is frankly incomprehensible to me and comes in my critical view with too much Gaelic shrieking, but hey, I'm no connoisseur. There are sobs from all round the congregation.

Then the address from the Minister.

He talks of David's kindness, his inherent humanity, his decency and his generosity. No one can take issues with any of this and there's a general swelling of the sob level from all corners of the Kirk as his virtues are further explored. I wonder what Alison and indeed Kathlyn make of this.

It's a human trait of course. Even bad people have some favourable press at their own funeral. And David was by no means one of the bad guys. But the sanctification of the dead has always troubled me. It's a kind of post-mortal airbrushing that goes on where the warts are removed and perfectly normal folk, with their usual collection of human flaws, are packed off to wherever we believe they are to go, with almost saintly behavioural traits bestowed upon them.

It's my turn next. I am introduced as David's oldest friend and I walk in as dignified a manner as I possibly can to the front of the church, turn and face the congregation.

I had considered saying a few words of my own about David's inherent decency but I decide against this on the grounds that this was not my place in this ceremony. So, I began with the reading.

'For everything there is a season, and a time for every matter under heaven: a time to be born, and a time to die; a time to plant, and a time to pluck up what is planted; a time to kill, and a time to heal.'

I surprise myself. I get through it without stumbling.

It's moving stuff indeed. As Kathlyn had suggested, perhaps a tad clichéd nowadays, but its poetry resonates regardless of one's attitude to Christianity generally and the Old Testament in particular. I have delivered the correct words unerringly to the tear-stained faces of David's children in the front row. I performed for them and for them only.

Mischievously it did occur to me mid-flow to change the wording to see if anyone was listening. 'A time to trade currency, a time to trade bonds; a time to pile into hedge funds, a time to pillage the weaker members of the Eurozone.' I think I may have got away with it, but quite rightly steered away from such provocation.

I leave the somewhat unwanted limelight and take my seat beside the fragrant Jana. 'You read well,' she says and pats my arm.

A couple more readings, another hymn and it's time to leave, following the still lamenting piper.

There are a few nods of acknowledgement as we stand outside the Kirk ready for the next stage of the ceremony. Cigarettes are lit in relief, mine included, and then the modern day phenomenon as people take their phones out, switch them on and check for emails and messages, as if in the hour they've just been away from their work something will have happened, something that needs their urgent attention will have passed. Worse still, they may have missed the opportunity to amass yet more money.

A few walk off concentrating, phone to their ear talking to their offices, aware that this is vaguely inappropriate what with Jesus' bit of history with temples and moneylenders – but hey, they're movers and shakers and the moving and the shaking of the modern world verily relies on this. I think sadly David would probably have understood.

Kathlyn comes over with the kids, looking sallow, in tow. 'Thank you Jamie,' she says, and plants a gentle kiss on my cheek. 'That meant a lot to me and the children.'

I say nothing, moved.

Cigarettes and calls to the IMF over, the congregation decant in their luxury cars across Edinburgh to the municipal oven that is at Warriston Crematorium. I haven't been here since my own parents were processed – but it is as I recall it, a soulless place which does not encourage much reverie on the meaning of life or indeed death. It's simply a dead body processing factory. The chapel is of course full, Alison is still here with her entourage in tow. Will she dare come back to the Golf Club for drinks and sandwiches? I sincerely hope not.

One more hymn and then the committal. The curtain moves around the flag-draped coffin and that is it, the party is over. We file out into the light Edinburgh sunshine, cigarettes and mobile communication handsets once again burst in to life and muffled conversations begin once more.

I stand with Jana unsure what to do or say.

We admire the flowers and queue to console the family. A couple of strangers shake my hand and thank me for my contribution. They glance at the same time, admiringly (the men) or disapprovingly (the women) in Jana's direction. I feel I could, perhaps should, explain my relationship with this particularly lovely product of Krakow (stoppit, OK?) but I rather like the envy and sense of mystery my close association with her is bestowing upon me.

People are milling around, waiting to leave, but worried about the protocol of being seen to head to the buffet too soon. And then I notice a woman looking at me.

She's about ten yards away, seemingly in the company of a group of people – but I can tell she's not engaged because she's patently not listening to the post funeral conversation. She's medium height with a round elfin face, jet-black hair framing her pretty face, large dark eyes discretely made up, and a somewhat voluptuous mouth nearly, but not quite, too big for her small face. She's wearing a simple black silk trouser suit and a plain white blouse which makes her stand out somewhat amongst the more formally-dressed other women, all high heels and funeral-chic designer cuts.

She smiles as she walks over to me. I smile back, aware that I should know who she is but unable to place her. But now I am rather enjoy being the object of her smile and determined to enjoy it for as long as possible.

'Jamie,' she says shaking my hand and planting a soft kiss on my cheek. Her perfume is something natural, not the harsh chemical brews of the great and good around her. There's rose and peach and orange in there – a lot to absorb from that momentary embrace. 'My big brother's good-looking friend'. And she fixes that smile on me once more.

'Emily,' I say. 'David's wee sister. Do you know Jana?' She nods and they embrace consoling each other.

I look Emily up and down. 'So you're all grown-up. You've ... changed.'

I'm tongue-tied and she knows it and quickly says 'Just as well I guess. If I'd stayed as a nine-year-old I'd be on the front page of *The Lancet* by now.' And she smiles again and her smile takes me out of the solemnity of the occasion and surroundings.

I remember now, I was twelve or so and she a lowly eight or nine, and therefore didn't register as a human being. She was just someone's kid sister who occasionally tagged along with us when David's mum instructed him to look after her. I recall a whingy brat, who would irritate us and grass David up to his parents if he upset her in any way.

And then at David's wedding I remember she was there, all spikes and dark makeup and bondage pants a good few years after the punk look had fizzled out. She'd spent the entire reception in the corner with some other Sid Vicious lookalike, ignored by all and sundry. She's just seemed ridiculous. Now looking at her smiling relaxed face, she seemed far from ridiculous.

'I had no idea I had made such an impact,' I say giving her my best smile.

'Oh Jamie,' she says sweetly, 'you were certainly top of the Barnton tops, with those tank tops and those flared jeans and that long hair. But to be fair, my brother's friends were somewhat plug-ugly, so you were the best of a moderately ugly bunch. Your supremacy amongst us truly pre-pubescents lasted, I believe, just three months. Then Alan arrived and you and your Mark Bolan curls were toast, I recall.'

I laugh. 'Bit like Mr Bolan himself,' I say and

regret it immediately – but she does smile. 'Story of my life,' I plough on, 'Second best in Barnton: to your brother at sport and to Alan in the looks department.'

I like Emily, I think to myself. She's interesting, she's quick-witted and clever, and not intimidated one jot by me or the circumstances in which she finds herself.

And fuck I even remember Alan arriving with his blond tousled hair and his Manchester accent, his bush-baby eyes and his penchant for soft (all you could get in those days) porn and his desire to smoke as many fags as he could steal from his parents.

'I think Alan's here,' she says. 'Kathlyn said he was coming. Now he was truly dreamy.' She smiles at me again.

'Oh go on,' I say faux seriously. 'Rub it in why don't you?'

I'm a tad torn. I remember Alan as a complete bastard, a Manc psychopath. He made me smoke a pack of cigarettes one afternoon when I didn't want to, which apparently would prove to the assembled kids that I wasn't a – as the vernacular of the day would have said – a poof. I did so and threw up on the way home, then got grounded by my mum who could smell tobacco on me. Similarly with cans of beer. Alan had a theory about my sexuality and he would stack all the evidence against me to prove that theory. So I drank cans of Tennent's lager that made my stomach turn just somehow to prove my heterosexuality.

I'd do anything to shut the bastard up because there was no alternative. I couldn't tell my mum or dad as they wouldn't have understood. So I flung myself off a twenty-foot parapet; I ran on to the golf course and stole a ball from the middle of the fourth fairway, causing two burly golfers to chase after me cursing and threatening me with a sound beating. He was a control freak but apparently everything I did under his control only went to show what a poof I was.

My reverie seems to have been noticed. 'You're hurt, bless you,' she says laughing a little, but she strokes my arm gently as she does. 'It still matters to you what we thought of you a hundred years back,' she says, a little too perceptively for my liking.

'Well I'd like to have kept some sex-god status in someone's memory at least, but I guess it was obviously never meant to be. Thank you, Emily, for both building me up and then destroying me so, in just five minutes. You verily are a star. I look forward to cowering in the shadow once more of Alan, if only to disprove finally his theories about my sexuality.'

I smile as I say this. And she smiles back.

'Sorry,' she says. 'I'm being ridiculously trivial teasing you like that. I should be looking sad, it's my brother's funeral after all'. And she laughs nervously. 'Of course I am sad. He was my bro after all and I loved him.' And sad she looks. And vulnerable and beautiful.

'If it's any consolation,' I say, 'you always were bloody irritating even then.'

'See,' she says, throwing her head back in laughter, 'neither of us have changed a bit!'

People join us, people she knows and people who seem to know me. She gives them all the same full-on smile, the same sad face when her loss is mentioned, but all along she seems gently bemused. She turns down my offer of a cigarette. 'Too early to indulge in such a vice,' she says and smiles at me again.

A smile that could melt autumn mist, I muse. That could render volcanic rock asunder – a smile that could both set every bird in the fecund woods singing ... and stop them again in their arboreal tracks. And that smile is, it appears, only for me. It has my name tattooed on the side of it. Her smile is directly sent to me, I decide.

A fat middle-aged bloke with a Friar Tuck thing going on top of his head approaches me looking sad. 'You won't remember me,' he says. He sticks his hand out and I shake it. 'Alan,' he says. 'Alan Whyte. We were kids together, way back when.' I shake my head, feigning memory loss.

'Alan,' I say, then, ' Oh, *Alan*. I remember now. Alan.' I look at him stone-faced.

He looks confused, perhaps scared even then

blurts out 'I just wanted to say how much I admired your reading. Brilliant. I couldn't do that. I'd have choked, well done.' He's still got the faintest hint of a nasal Mancunian accent in behind the Edinburgh burr.

'Not so much a poof after all, I guess,' I say and as I do so I cannot resist smiling angelically at both Emily and Jana, (who has appeared by my side once more after an obviously productive visit to the bar).. 'Shall we go?' I say to Jana and turn on my heel

Sometimes, I think as we walk to the car, I am utterly pathetic. I still hold a grudge against a bloke that I actually don't know, because of something he did – long forgotten by him by now, I am sure – some forty plus years ago.

As we walk to the car, I try to explain to Jana my actions. She's not terribly supportive. First off I have to explain the word 'poof' and in doing so I also have to explain that it's not a nice word and it's not used nowadays. In 1970s Britain, it was commonplace as was homophobia. In the car as we head off we have a rather confusing (for both of us I believe) conversation about my actual sexuality.

I thought I was doing very well until she says, 'You should come out, Jamie. This is twenty-first century, not 1950s. You gay – you be proud'.

We spent the rest of the journey to the funereal reception with her teaching me the basics of gay rights. 'Be proud, Jamie,' she says a tad too loudly I think, as we enter the Golf Club bar area. 'Nothing wrong with being gay!' Mourners' heads definitely turn at this juncture and I do wonder, briefly, how much things have actually changed in terms of sexual politics in this particular neck of the woods. 'You be proud,' and with that she kisses me firmly on the cheek.

Extraordinary how complicated my life can be sometimes.

I look around me. It's a vast ballroom overlooking presumably the eighteenth green and out across the well-manicured course. I've never played the course (I refer you to my earlier golfing theories, thoughts and exploits) or even stepped foot in here before. My politics and golf game were never up to it. There's half of Birnam Wood been cut down to supply the oak panelling. There are plaques on the wall denoting winners of various competitions going back many years, and photographs of famous competitors of decades gone by. The carpet and curtains are of a dark tartan design.

This is one of the headquarters of the Edinburgh, actually Scottish, supposed social elite – the place where friendships have been sealed and betrayed over the years, deals done and reneged upon. It's fusty, it smacks of ill-deserved privilege and it is definitely heading towards top of the list of places I will burn if, or indeed when, I get my fucking act together and start a Marxist revolution (after hiding a few quid offshore, obviously).

The room gradually fills up with besuited and bekilted men, talking discreetly and helping themselves to glasses of wine or whisky from the trays proffered by the waiters and waitresses. And I know that the only thing which will get me through this afternoon is to drink proficiently and steadily, achieving a gentle level of drunkenness that only I shall be aware of. It's a plan and a damn fine one in my book, and I start on the wine.

I'm halfway through my third glass when David's kids arrive. They thank me again for my contribution and Kathlyn kisses me on the cheek and thanks me too. 'David would have appreciated that,' she says.

'It was nothing,' I say modestly. 'A beautiful service,' I comment because that's what you're supposed to say in these circumstances. She's swiftly taken over by some banking dignitary and I am left there with the kids unsure what to say. 'Do you play golf at all Calum?' I ask the lad lamely.

'Not really,' he says. 'Dad was so good I never wanted to try to compete. He played off something stupid like three.' He would, wouldn't he? I think to myself. The girl is just standing looking bored. A tray of white wine is carried past her and she swiftly grabs one.

'Mum will go mad!' says Calum.

'Fuck her,' says the girl and swigs half the glass down in one.

'Right!' says Calum grabbing a whisky off a tray. He tries to knock it back in one but its patently obvious he's a newcomer and it sticks a little in his throat. He coughs a bit then does manage to down it.

I look around in mild panic. I confess to being a bit crap when it came to my parenting skills when my kids were this age, so I don't feel any confidence in my ability to deal with this particular situation.

Kirsty finishes her drink and they both look around for the arrival of the next.

'Look,' I say calmly, 'don't be fucking arseholes at your dad's funeral.' They both look at me in shock. I infer genteel Edinburgh society does not usually utter such expressions. They should, in my humble opinion.

'If you both drink wine and Scotch you'll be carried out and that would be humiliating. In fact I won't allow that to happen. I shall call the manager and tell them you're underage drinkers and he'll bar you and probably call the cops and the bar staff will go to prison as will your mum. OK?'

'OK,' they say sulkily, not believing my narrative, I suspect.

'Good, so let's be sensible. You Calum can have a beer. What would you like Kirsty?' She settles on a pear cider. I have a discrete word with the waiter and the drinks appear.

'Now be sensible,' I say. 'If you want another you find me and I will organise. Those are the rules – OK?'

They nod obediently and I think I have found a couple of fans. 'Oh and if anyone asks you're drinking shandy and you lemon and lime – OK?'

They smile complicitly .

I down my glass in one and swiftly take another. Yes, I do recognise my hypocrisy and poor example-setting, thank you ...

I look around the room which is now virtually full. There's a low respectful murmur of conversation humming throughout. I overhear snippets. 'He was a very lucky boy on that deal, I tell you. He could have crashed the Hang Seng there and then.' 'I emailed him – get into gold. But I'd mistyped – it was late and I'd had a couple, I confess. He thought I was telling him to get into God. Lord knows where his portfolio would be now.' And wittily 'The Euro's ripe for plunder. If we're not aggressive and crash it some Yank will be, you mark my words.' All the time I'm scanning the room looking for Emily.

These people – these wealthy, smug, rich upper-middle-class people with their private schools for the kids, and skiing lodges, and affairs with the au pair, and three BMWs – run this country. They brought it to its knees just a couple of years back but we, the ordinary people, baled them out so that they can continue doing exactly what it was they were doing before, and feathering their own Cramond and Morningside, Kensington and Chelsea, nests. I mean at least mill and mine owners of the nineteenth century actually made things and got wealthy on manufacturing or trade. OK it was at the expense of the exploited working classes and that was unforgivable. (Although when do you hear the word 'philanthropist' nowadays, except when talking to a dyslexic stamp collector? Because at least a few of those Victorians provided housing and some education to their workers. Imagine that now ...?) If the definition of madness is to keep doing the same thing and expecting different outcomes, then that's exemplified by the people in this room who always come up smelling of rose petals while the normal folk, the people serving the food and wine here, for example, can barely afford a roof over their heads and always smell of manure. OK, so our working classes don't risk their lives (often) or limb loss from a Spinning Fucking Jenny (I know nothing, I confess, of the workings of the Spinning Jenny and so I'm but guessing on their potential collateral damage but please substitute your own Industrial Revolutionary death-trap bit of kit here if you so choose) – but their jobs, houses and livelihoods disappear because of the fuck ups this bunch of pricks make.

'Ghastly. Fucking ghastly,' says a voice at my elbow and Emily is there, smiling up at me.

'Oh indeed,' I say. 'The only consolation is that if your brother was here, he'd probably be very flattered to see quite so many of the great and the good of Scottish society turning out to drink on his tab.'

'Maybe latterly,' she says. 'But that wasn't him really. That was what he became, trying to do and be the right thing. Just ... trying to blend in. But deep down I think he was a free spirit.'.

'Well I for one plan to celebrate the poor bastard's life by getting utterly shit-faced. Care to join me?'

'Don't mind if I do,' she says smiling, and we both grab a glass of wine each.

'So Emily, what do you do? In fact, what have you been doing since you were that irritating little kid a hundred years ago?' I ask her.

She begins to tell me. She'd taken a law degree in Glasgow 'Fuck knows why. Boring as hell, but I thought it might please my mum and dad.'

'Did it?'

'It did,' she says, 'Very much. I graduated, just about, having perhaps over-indulged in having fun. Somehow ended up in property law and benefited from the great building boom in Edinburgh of the early and mid-nineties.' She reels off various developments in the city that she's worked on. 'Fucking terrible,' she said. 'Glass, brutalist monstrosities that we were paid a fortune to make sure they got planning permission for. Whenever I come back I feel ashamed.'

Then she fell in love with a young architect. 'Dunno why, just fell for him.' She looks momentarily sad, remembering. 'He was a good-looking lad. I always went for the good-looking ones. We set up home, a flat in the old town. My mum and dad were really proud then. Love's young dream. Then it went rather tits up.'

'Why?' I asked.

'Turned out that brutalist monstrosities weren't the only thing he was interested in erecting. He was travelling all over Scotland while I was going home each day playing the wee wifey. And one day he told me he'd been shagging a town planner from Bearsden called Nathalie and that he was moving in with her.'

'I'm sorry,' I say. 'I know how that feels.'

'What, you've shagged Nathalie from Bearsden too?' she asks innocently and wide-eyed and we both laugh.

I tell her of my own marital experience. Well part of it. I didn't think she needs to know that I had recently been shagging my ex-wife.

Now she lives on the outskirts of Pitlochry, Emily tells me. 'Arse end of nowhere. Love it.'

'Are you still practising law?'

'Not really as such, ' she says. 'I'm very right on,

don't ya know? I work for a number of ecology charities. Skint of course,' she says, 'but happy and fulfilled.'

We clink glasses, finish the drink and snatch another two.

'Tell me more,' I say. I like talking to this woman very much.

'Well, they're fucking the countryside big time. Salmon farms that kill the native fish. Estates owned by billionaires that produce nothing but pheasant and grouse for rich folk to shoot. Poison the raptors. Fucks the natural countryside big time.' She's warming to her theme. 'Just over four hundred folk own about half of rural Scotland. Imagine that – it's obscene. And they don't do so in the main to protect it. I'm writing a book about it.'

'Have you got a publisher?' I ask.

Suddenly Alan's beside us. 'Jamie,' he says, 'I know earlier you were upset but I'll say it again. Well done. Great reading. David would be proud of you.'

'Thanks, Alan,' I say, 'Appreciate that.'

We shake hands and he pats me on the back as we do so. I realise that this middle-aged, balding self-important twat of a bloke bears no resemblance to the kid who used to taunt me. He probably doesn't even remember the taunting. I need to learn to live and let live, I think.

A couple of other middle-aged guys ship up and

introduce themselves. I vaguely remember them from my youth and we swap memories of David and sixties' summers. Emily engages with them as little as she can.

Then Jana appears and it's pretty obvious she's had a drink or fifteen. 'You bastard,' she says forcibly to Alan. 'So what he gay? He nice man and this twenty-first century. You be ashamed, bastard,' and she takes my arm protectively.

Even Emily's been struck dumb. 'Erm, language problem, I believe,' I say apologetically. 'Wrong end of the sti...'

'See you bastard,' Jana continues. 'Make him deny what he is. Shame on you.'

Alan looks confused, the others awkward. Emily is looking at me with a puzzled smile.

'Jana,' I say. 'Please.'

'You Scottish, you too polite!' and with that she was off in search of another drink.

'I could explain,' I say to the stunned group 'but frankly I cannot be arsed. Emily,' I say, 'do you fancy a smoke outside?'

'Jamie, I do indeed,' she says and takes my arm. We leave the group and she manages to ask between giggles 'What the fuck was that all about?'

I explain as we descend the vast staircase. We go out through the grand carved front doors and I stop to light a cigarette. 'Tell you what,' she says, 'let's be really naughty,' and with that she leads me round the side of the vast building.

Yes, Dear Reader, momentarily I think what you are probably thinking, that she's trying to lure me for a knee-trembler in the groundsman's hut. But no. We go to the side of the groundsman's hut that's true, but no carnality ensues. Instead she takes out a pouch of tobacco, some filter papers and a small bag of dope. 'It's mild stuff,' she say.

She rolls a joint expertly, lights it and inhales, then blows a huge plume of smoke out. 'Enjoy,' she says, passing the joint (do people still call them joints? Tokes? C'mon, help me here!). Now, I remember my last dope-related experience ended in abject humiliation and I am keen not repeat it. So I cheat a wee bit, inhaling only a little, but enough to feel the effect. A pleasant mellowness kicks in through my body. I could get used to this, I think.

It feels naughty this hiding away, this conspiratorial behaviour with a beautiful younger woman. My friend's kid sister. We say nothing for a while, just thinking thoughts and looking over the slightly misty golf course in the early Edinburgh evening. There's a constant stream of planes a couple of hundred feet above us flying in to the airport. What a view they must have, of the cityscape one side and the Firth of Forth and bridges the other. It's a great city and one I feel at home in despite the fact I have been away for nearly forty years.

She takes a drag on the joint and passes it to me as she exhales. 'Sometimes,' she says 'it all just seems a little futile. I loved my brother. When I was a kid I idolised him.'

'And some of his older mates?' I interrupt and she smiles.

'Some of them,' she says and looks at me in what I take to be a tender way. 'You've certainly aged better than that tool Alan.'

'Damned with faint praise,' I say, passing back the diminishing joint.

There's a comfortable silence broken by her saying, 'I used to think David would always be there for me, that we'd always be close, that if ever I got into trouble he'd help me out. That was especially difficult as Mum and Dad went when I was so young.'

'Shit,' I think. I'd forgotten about their parents. They died in their early sixties, one of a swift cancer, one of a stroke months later. I recall I sent cards, that was all. Shit friend, me. Too busy to attend their funerals.

'And Christ, he did help me out,' she says smiling and passing the last of the joint to me. ' After my marriage ended, I was what is known in these genteel climes as fucking trouble. Men and drink and drugs. I actually got arrested a couple of times for possession. That's why I'm no longer a lawyer. I was a colossal fuck-up. But he was always there, a parent and a brother and I thought he'd be there for life. Selfish of me really.'

'You're lucky to have had someone so close,' I say, about to add, 'I never had', but I realise this is her moment to confide in me. And I should appreciate that privilege.

'Yup, but he did change after he met Kathlyn, though. Prim, proper Kathlyn. Butter wouldn't melt Kathlyn. Never warmed to me, that woman. Thought I'd embarrass her somehow.'

'She's been great with me the last few days,' I say, 'considering what she's going through. But I did wonder at the time what he saw in her. I mean, she was perfectly pleasant and attractive, but I never saw a spark between them.'

'Oh, I think he wanted respectability. Don't forget my mum and dad were working class, pulled themselves up by their boot straps and made good. Rough and ready. Unsophisticated. Kathlyn was class, or at least she thought she was. And that's what he fell for.'

'It happens, Emily,' I say.

'Well it should never have happened to my big brother, that's for sure,' and she starts to gently cry.

I don't know what to do, frankly. I'm stuck outside a greenkeeper's hut with a woman I've not seen since Margaret Thatcher was in power, and she's crying, and here I am fucking hesitating. I very gently put my arm around her and she nestles in.

We stand there for quite a long time and, Dear Reader, it felt good. No, not in a trouserly stirrings way – how superficial and shallow you must think I am – but in a natural this-is-what-human-beings-should-mean-to-each-other kind of way.

My head leans down towards hers and I smell the blossom in her hair. Oh, and a wee bit of dope.

It is this scenario that greets Calum and Kirsty as they come around the corner of the hut. They do a kind of double take, embarrassed, and Calum yells out 'Aunty Emily!' and Kirsty says, 'Jamie why are you kissing Aunty Emily?'.

'I'm not,' I say pathetically, trying to disentangle myself – and realising that this is the second time in a couple of weeks that I've seemingly been rumbled by a teenager for an act of public intimacy, only this time I am absolutely innocent of all charges, your honour – 'Aunty Emily was sad and I was trying to ...'

'Feel her up,' said Calum. I think he's had a wee bit more to drink than had been agreed.

Emily's face changes from sadness to laughter. 'You dirty wee bugger,' she says laughing. 'You should be ashamed of yourself saying that.' But she's still laughing. 'Bugger it and give me a hug.'

And the three of them hug and laugh and then cry, and I realise that this is the first sign of true human emotion I've seen all day.

'You can join in too,' says Kirsty.

'Thank you I will.'

The greenkeeper, about to head off to repair a bunker on the eighth, got the shock of his life as he came around the corner to his shed.

'Right, let's get back in to the merry fray and have some fun,' says Emily grabbing the kids by the arm.

'Aunty?' says Calum. 'Have you been smoking dope? I can smell it on you.'

'What does the Royal Academy teach you kids these days?' she says laughing and I follow them, swept along by the affection.

20. Ever Fallen in Love (With Someone You Shouldn't've)

The rest of the evening descends into surprisingly quite a fun time. As people drink more so their cliques break down. Various men of finance engage us in conversation and Emily essentially makes up lies. We are married, have been secretly for a couple of years. Then I am the husband of her lesbian lover and I have been caught having an affair with the greenkeeper here (having seen the greenkeeper earlier, this thought puts me off the canapés somewhat). We are platonic friends about to go across the Andes by yak. She just seems to open her mouth and fun, nonsense stuff pours out. The converse of this is that when she opens her mouth more alcohol seems to pour itself into mine. The more sober of the besuited fucks realise they are being pranked here and leave our company pretty quickly to find less challenging funereal colleagues, obviously shocked at the inappropriateness of Emily's behaviour. Some of the racier, more pissed fellows, stick around enjoying her vivacity and irreverence.

And me? I just stand and drink and watch this woman and realise that, if I am not very, very careful, I am probably going to fall scabby head over calloused heels in love with her, and that would probably be a very, very daft thing to do.

And then gradually as the evening dusk arrives on the skyline, the wake is finishing. People say their goodbyes, returning to their lives after pondering their mortality. Alan, a bit the worse for wear, comes over, kisses Emily and shakes my hand once more. My anger towards him has passed, mercifully, and thankfully Jana is nowhere to be seen to berate him for his four-decades old homophobia.

There are a handful of folk left: Kathlyn at the far end of the room looking fragile, tired and strained, surrounded by a few of the people who I recognise had been at the house earlier.

I catch her eye and she smiles. I smile back. The kids, having stayed with Emily pretty much the whole afternoon as she's been sneaking them (albeit watered down) drinks despite my warning, are beside their mother now. I join them, as does Emily.

'Right,' I say breezily aware it's time to go. 'What now?'

'A nightclub perhaps?' says Emily.

'I'm too old I'm afraid, and we'd never get the kids in ...' I begin to say before realising she's taking the piss again. She winks at me. I wish she wouldn't do that, truly. I think fears of falling for her big time should be taken seriously.

Taxis are called as no one is in a fit condition to drive the short distance back to the family home. Momentarily I wonder if Emily will head off somewhere else. She must have friends in the city and she's certainly no fan of Kathlyn, but no, she dutifully hops in a cab with the kids.

Kathlyn and I end up in the last cab together. She grabs my arm and pulls herself towards me.

'Thank you again for today,' she says solemnly. 'It was so lovely having someone who knew David for so long. It made all the difference.'

'Truly,' I say, 'it was nothing. I feel honoured to have been asked.'

'You're a good friend,' she says, patting my hand. 'I hope you stay one.'

'I will,' I say, a little embarrassed because I've been a piss-poor friend up until now.

'I saw her there, of course. The little bitch.' For a moment I think she's talking about Emily for some reason, but she goes on, 'Bloody Alison. I thought of asking you to kick her backside out of the Kirk, but that would have only made a scene. The papers would have loved it. There were journos from *The Scotsman* and the *Evening News* just waiting for something juicy to report. You wrestling with her over David's coffin would have done that.' She laughs weakly. 'We could have got on the front page if I'd not been such a coward.'

'Probably best you didn't,' I say sagely. 'For the kids' sake.'

'You're right. I did get word to her through one of David's underlings that if she stepped foot in the wake I would have her thrown out. And thankfully she did back off. She didn't dare show her face.'I say nothing and the taxi bounds up the hill to the family house. As we pull into the drive I go to open the door. 'A word, Jamie,' she says. 'I don't know you well, but I count you as a friend. Be careful of Emily. I saw you spend most of your time with her this afternoon. I understand why.' She touches my arm. 'She has certain charms. Men like her.'

'I thought she was great fun,' I begin to say but she cuts me off.

'She's dangerous, trust me,' she says. 'She's had a lot of relationships and it's always Emily that ends them.' This doesn't tally with the Bearsden slapper narrative but I hold my tongue. 'It's the men that get hurt. Be careful, that's all. I know you're vulnerable.'

And with that we get out of the taxi and I pay, thinking I feel anything but vulnerable right now. I feel invigorated, I feel challenged, I feel attracted and most of all I feel more alive than I can remember feeling for years.

There are twenty or so people at the house. Cups of tea and coffee are proffered but I simply help myself to a glass of wine. I find the kids and sit with them. They're distractedly watching some reality TV shite on the telly. Women in bikinis and guys in speedos sitting around a villa pool

Kirsty says to me, 'Aunt Emily is brilliant, isn't she eh?' And Calum concurs. 'Were you snogging?' she asks.

'Don't be impertinent,' I say calmly. 'Of course not. I was just comforting her. Men of my age do not snog.'

Calum points at the TV where a clinically-enhanced large-breasted blonde woman is getting out of a pool. 'I bet you'd snog her, Jamie ...'

'I think perhaps Calum we should maybe turn this nonsense off, don't you? And doesn't your ridiculously expensive school teach you to avoid this kind of rubbish?'

'It's just a bit of fun,' he says, switching the TV off with the remote control. 'Dad never let us watch that kind of stuff. Sport or documentaries, that was him.' He looks sad again and I think how stupid I've been in not letting him escape into the swimwear idyll. He's got the rest of his life to miss his dad, another few minutes of deflection would not have hurt.

We chat for a little longer and I leave them. They look washed out, in need of their beds after such a day while I need another cigarette. I want to hook up with Emily again but I can't see where she's gone. After what Kathlyn said it may well be that my interest is a little too obvious and so, for my dignity's sake, I am determined to play it a little cooler than I have been so far. But the truth of the matter is that I don't want to be cool with her. I'm just sensitive to the fact that hunting down my oldest friend's younger sister and trying to persuade her to spend the rest of her life with me, might be deemed a little – oh how shall I put it? – impetuous, inappropriate at the moment, and downright fucking stupid.

So I exit through the baronial front door and step onto the lawn.

I light up and stare into the evening sky. The planes stream past still, even at this time of the evening, and I am suddenly overcome with fatigue. It has been a long day. I finish the cigarette and immediately light another. This is folly I think, and I'm not talking about chain-smoking. Emily is a mere temporary infatuation. I shall wake in the morning hung-over, embarrassed and ready to head south to the world that is really my home. Scotland isn't. It's the dream of the homeland only: the kind of dream that gets thousands of Canadians to turn up in kilts at North American Highland Games and make jokes while they toss their cabers. This place is no better to live in than anywhere else on the globe. I left here a million years ago. Yes, it has left its mark on me; yes, I have fond memories of it; and yes, it is a magnificent city (OK, if you forget the rain) but I am but passing through.

If I did move here, would I find peace, happiness even? No. The physical environment isn't going to sort out my malcontentedness – my contempt for others but mainly for myself. I'd just be fucked-up Jamie only 400 miles further north than when I was at peak fuck-up. Helen, Christine, even Emily sadly, are not going to bring happiness to this guy, that's for sure.

I walk around the garden enjoying the late evening dampness. There's a small burn running at the bottom and for some reason I remember its gurgling song from one particular bike ride many years ago. There had been six or eight of us from the street I lived in then, out on a local adventure as we did often. We stopped because one of the kids, and actually I think it was David, had nearly run a small frog over. We had gathered round it excitedly and – after some consternation – I, as the eldest, was nominated to pick it up and place it somewhere safe. Trying to hide my amphibian-related fear and revulsion, I had lifted it into the palm of one hand. I could feel its heartbeat and I, brave in front of my younger mates, had then got a wee bit cocky. I pretended to pop it down the back of one kid's shirt, then to dash it on the road. All the time I felt the animal alive in my hand.

I wasn't a cruel kid and after a minute or so, I realised it should be released. Someone mentioned that fifty yards down the road there was a burn.

Ceremoniously we walked there and I released the frog into the water.

It was the same burn that I am looking at now. I even remember David saying that one day he'd live in a house with a burn at the bottom of the garden. He'd obviously achieved that particular dream.

I finish the cigarette and contemplate throwing it into the water but momentarily become concerned at the carcinogenic effect it may have on the relatives of my frog friend from several generations back. This last memory – of something that happened over forty years ago, that has come from nowhere after being hidden all that time – has for some reason made exhaustion hit me. I'm done in and I resolve to go to bed with no further ado.

I turn towards the house and Emily is standing three yards from me. I wonder how long she's been there. I walk up to her and she takes my arm. We walk back to the house in silence.

I do the rounds of saying good night, starting with Emily who is now seated on the sofa staring into space, and finish with the kids. I say to them simply 'Anytime you want to talk to me, any advice I can give, just call me,' and self-consciously give them both my business card. 'My phone and email addresses are on here.' I hug them both. As we pull away, I add in a whisper, 'Anytime you want to get shit-faced – when you're a wee bit older of course –

in England with my kids you know where we are.' They smile.

The house seems to be emptying as I climb the baronial staircase, with its mix of expensive contemporary art-collages and abstracts and metalwork sculptures suspended on the wall, combined with David's romantic scenes from the Highland Clearances. Fortunately the house is so fucking big and solidly built, I'm not going to be disturbed by the comings and goings from downstairs.

I go into the room, have a pee, but am too tired for the usual wash of face, oxters and teeth. But I do remember that I have a couple of nips of Scotch left and think that I probably need a nightcap in solitary confinement in order to take in the enormity of the day.

So I lie in bed in a T-shirt and my pants, with a glass of cheap, blended Scotch feeling a wee bit like I was in a working-class flat in Drylaw, not in one of the most sought-after houses in Edinburgh.

I think back over the day. Of Jana and my sexuality, of my utter revulsion of the men of money. Fucking idiot, I think. They can't all have been financiers. In that social circle there would have been medical consultants, lawyers and barristers. I realise with just a hint of self-loathing that my prejudices are pretty broad-reaching and – when I felt uncomfortable with, and downright judgemental of, the lowland Scot's scene, all refined, perfectly harmonious, Edinburgh gentility, all Sunday-supplement, Audi-driving sensitivities and absolute respectability – it was actually me I was judging. How many of them, like David, wanted something different; how many would have been happier unbuttoned with someone warm and alive such as Emily, rather than buttoned-up like Kathlyn?

And now of course I allow myself to think of Emily. How she smiles somehow with just her eyes, how her jaw juts confidently when she speaks, how her mouth is full and sensuous and her neck just arches, ready to be kissed. And guess what, Dear Reader? Trouserly, well strictly speaking, boxerly (you old pedant) stirrings occur.

I have – if you have followed my travails over the last few years, dear and only true friend – a tendency to become infatuated quickly with women then bored shortly after. Like most blokes I want what I can't have, and on the rare occasions I end up getting what I shouldn't have, I don't want it anymore. The mind of a three-year-old trapped in the usually flaccid body of a middle-aged bloke, it's true.

And she's my dead mate's kid sister – albeit a beautiful late-forties kid sister – with a laugh that could melt polar ice if global warming has left any of it behind to be melted. I have one of my flashing visions: when a long period of time passes in seconds through my mind and a scenario covering several years blinks its message to me in a nanosecond. I've wooed her and won her and we've married and we live in the country together, and we make love frequently and laugh continuously and talk passionately and need each other frantically.

'Fuck,' I say to myself knocking back the Scotch and pouring the remains of the bottle into my glass. 'You've fallen in love you utter, utter knobhead.'

I finish the drink and switch the light off. And continue thinking of Emily, which means much-needed sleep eludes me but I know how to handle this. When stressed or anxious in the past, I have mental games I play that are so knob-numbingly tedious that they send me to sleep within minutes. I have just got to Lima in my 'Alphabetical Capital Cities/Countries of the World' game (I suspect Waddington's will be on to this one in a flash) and I'm beginning to drift off when there's a light tap on the door.

The light tap could be gunshots from where I'm lying such is the jolt they cause me, and before I can respond I hear the door open. A refined Edinburgh voice whispers 'Jamie, I've wanted you for so long. Take me up the Carse of Gowrie' and as I fumble for the light switch, which of course I cannot fucking find, I say in panic 'Kathlyn, no this isn't right!' and as

I do, I switch the light on and there's Emily creased up with laughter in front of the bed.

'Oh, you should be so lucky to think Ms Jean Brodie,' (this in a passable Maggie Smith accent) 'might be after you'.

'Oh stranger things have happened, I can assure you,' I say still a little shocked and trying to cover my bare legs with the duvet. And then I laugh too.

She's wearing a Scottish rugby shirt from a few years back. I can tell this because it's without any advertising logo. It's probably David's. It's baggy and it comes to just above her knee and I think there and then, that I have never seen anyone quite so beautiful in all my life. Well, not in a Scottish rugby shirt at least.

'Don't take this the wrong way,' she says, 'but David's baby sis needs a cuddle'. We look at each other and she drops the little girl lost look. 'Seriously. I always make it a habit not to get laid in my brother's house, at least on the day of his funeral. I'm old-fashioned like that. But in this,' she groped for words, 'mausoleum, I don't think I can be alone tonight. Can you be a gentleman?'

'Yes,' says my mouth. 'Fuck off,' counter my genitals.

I pull back the covers and she climbs in beside me. I put my arm around her, her blossom-smell pervading my senses.

'Och,' she said in her best Hawick accent, 'just

imagine I'm Willie John McBride. That'll dampen your ardour.'

'He was Irish,' I state.

'Bugger,' she says in her normal voice. 'Is it only Irish rugby players you're attracted to?' Then again in her posh Edinburgh accent, 'So was there just the wee-est grain of truth in what Alan said all those years ago?'

'Christ you're as fucking annoying as you were all those years back.'

We chat inanely like this, like teenage lovers actually, for some considerable time.

Then she says, 'If you snore, you'll wake up without nostrils. Goodnight, Jamie.'

I kiss her gently on her head and say goodnight.

At about six she wakes, kisses me chastely on the cheek and says, 'Goodbye big bruv's handsome friend. Thank you. I'd better leave before,' and this in a wild Highland voice, 'the parrush gets tae hear!'

I smile, 'Can I at least get your number?' I ask.

'Bad idea' she says. 'Very bad idea.'

'Why?' I ask. I realise we're talking in whispers.

'Because you might fall in love.'

'Might I?' I ask. 'And you won't?'

'Nope. Too old. Too bruised. Distrustful. Fickle. Polyamorous. You're a nice man. You don't need me.'

'It might be fun trying,' I say.

'Fun's fine,' she says, frowning. She still looks

gorgeous, I think, even when frowning. She breaks my reverie by continuing, 'Until it stops being fun and real life gets in the way. As it always does. And certainly will in this case.' She looks at me and smiles a little sadly.

'You missed 'cynical' out of that list of adjectives. Look – just give me your number. We should stay in touch. For David's sake. Where's the harm?'

'There was a time I think I actually used to appall him, the firebrand sister, the rebel.' She pauses, thinking, more fleeting sadness once more. 'The drugs, the blokes. What might his friends think? What would your friends think?'

'That you're smart. And beautiful. Obviously a pain in the backside, and fucking irritating, but really rather lovely.'

She looks at me. 'Oh what the fuck,' she says. There's a pen and a notepad on the bureau and she scribbles a number down. 'Pointless, absolutely pointless,' she mutters. 'You're in Surrey ...'

'Kent,' I correct her.

'It's all sarf to me,' she says in a passable Cockney accent.

'Well who knows what might happen?' I say.

'See you over breakfast,' she says and she leaves very quietly. I smile.

I lie in bed captivated. And very horny.

Epilogue – You Can't Always Get What You Want

We approach the end of my story, the more literarily discerning of you may be delighted to hear. Five years have passed and so much has happened. And at the same time, mercifully, so little.

Emily and I parted the day after the funeral, in a way that was designed specifically to quash any suspicion of Kathlyn and her children, that we had spent the night together – no matter how chastely we had achieved that. And who would believe anyway that Emily knew the concept of chastity? Her reputation in that family preceded her. So I kissed her on the cheek after breakfast and said 'It was lovely to see you again, take very good care of yourself, Emily'. She caught my eye and swiftly suppressed a half smile.

'And you, Jamie,' she said deadpan. 'Thanks for all you have done for the family. David would have approved of the care and comfort you gave us all.' And here she did actually wink at me. 'Safe journey home back to Surrey.'

'It's Kent actually,' I say as she walks towards the door of the dining room. She turns round, winks and pokes her tongue out at me.

I didn't want her to leave, but I couldn't stop her.

Next was Kathlyn. 'Thanks Jamie, you've been such a comfort to us all.' We hugged chastely. There was an awful lot of chastity around that morning, a chastity belt in fact, like a Green Belt ... only more chaste. 'You've been a good friend.'

'I've been no such thing,' I said. 'I didn't see David enough and now it's too late.' I was genuinely emotional and turned my face away to hide the fact that I was tearful. 'I've been so self-absorbed, I've not recognised what's important in my life.'

'We all do that,' she said quietly. 'I wonder what pressure I put on him and how I affected his health over his stupid affair. Christ, I put him through the wringer over that. Did he deserve those years of punishment? He was just a guy, a good man who slipped, and perhaps if I'd been more forgiving ...'

'You actually can't think like that,' I interrupted her. 'He was appalled at his weakness – I know that. Your response was natural and he knew that too. The fact he dug in to try to save the marriage says how much he loved you.'

She cried. I held her. I cried too. It was the first feeling of loss, of true sorrow I'd experienced throughout the last couple of days. Finally with all the bureaucracy of death done and eternally dusted, I could grieve for someone I had known for all but five years of my life.

'I should have been a better friend,' I told her. 'I was just too big a fucking narcissist. The world revolved around dear old Jamie, and if it didn't, I wanted to know why not.' I paused, thinking of Helen, my children, the boozing, the cigarettes, the self-pity, the treating my body and mind like they were replaceable or disposable, and said out loud but mainly to myself, 'I have to change'. And do you know what, Dear Reader? I fucking meant it.

I said my final goodbyes and drove out through the colossal fortification that was their front gate, out past the row of shops of my youth, and left Edinburgh with nary a look back. I drove south thinking constantly, stopping only for a sandwich and the loo. I thought of David and of my petty jealousy stretching back over the years. Could I have done more, could I have actually been a better friend?

Of course not, I had concluded by the time I reached Carlisle. He had a heart attack and died. The only way I could have stopped that happening would have been had I trained as a cardiologist rather than winging a career as a publisher – but I didn't. The truth is, I told myself as the motorway climbed up passed Shap, David had died and there's nothing I or anyone could do to alter that fact. But I recognised that I had missed years of his friendship because I simply couldn't fit it in to my busy schedule of self-loathing.

At Preston, the slightest inkling of a plan presented itself to me. I ruminated on until I saw the signs for Stoke-on-Trent, which I ignored (a wise move for anyone). It was then I realised I had to develop said plan and act on it. Not now, not straight away, not on impulse – but when I had considered it properly and deeply. If I was not on the road to Damascus I was on the road passing Royal Leamington Spa when I accepted that the plan was workable, wise, considered and deliverable.

One word. One proper noun. Coloured by improper thoughts, granted.

Emily.

No do not be quite so quick to judge me, Gentle Reader. Sure, in the time you've known and listened to my inane but decidedly heartfelt outpourings regarding Helen, Christine, Lizzie and the rest, you would be within your rights absolutely to think that once again my testes were controlling what my brain should have been looking after.

Not so this time.

She'd captivated me, the hippy boho dress sense, the wicked sense of humour, the irresponsible behaviour and reluctance to act her age. Did I love her? No idea. But I wanted to find out. Was she interested in money, mine or anyone else's? Nope, of that I was certain. Would she make me happy? Probably not. Would it be fun finding out? Possibly.

That night together had been so utterly innocent, so charming, so uncomplicated without the exchange of guilt-ridden bodily fluids, that I wanted to experience it again. And again.

I would be her friend, I could be there for her, if she wanted me to be. She would make me laugh – she'd probably make me cry but I knew she was authentic, uncomplicated (no actually scrub that, she's nothing if not fucking complicated) and just fun to be around. If it was more than that, if it turned into love, if it was intimate companionship then great – but it would be something significant, of that I was sure.

Passing High Wycombe, (as with Stoke-on-Trent, a wise move) the euphoria and excitement was a little dissipated. She lived in the wilds of Perthshire, I had to remind myself. She wouldn't move south and I certainly would not move north, despite the sometimes romantic hankering I had to leave forever the Garden of England and take up residence in God's own country/city. It just wasn't going to happen. I had a life in the South, I had kids who I wanted to be around as they grew in to adulthood, and get to know again to make up the lost time in my wilderness years of corporate slavery when we'd barely been on nodding terms.

You see? I was starting to become a better person already.

As I hit the M25 orbital car park the self-analysis was complete. I had reached a conclusion and that conclusion was that I think I had fallen in love with Emily precisely because I knew I couldn't have her. It was impossible, and therefore I was not going to emotionally martyr myself once more by clinging to the impossible.

And Dear Reader, you are probably saying to yourself what a presumptuous knobhead your friend Jamie has become. He had fallen in love with Emily or so he thought – but what of Emily? Was she pining amongst the Perthshire pine trees for this preposterous prick? Possibly – but probably not. With more baggage than a specialist luggage store on a retail park outside Wolverhampton, (by her own admission) she'd probably moved on emotionally already.

So, by the time I had arrived home – legs aching from sitting in a car designed for dwarfs – I had come to terms with my lot. Emily would have the very best of friends in her dead brother's best mate, and that would be all. Friends.

And those five years have truly flown by as years do as we reach middle age. The blink of an eye, the turning of a page and another year older and closer to decrepitude and meeting up with David for a glass or two of nectar.

Let me fill you in on what's been happening. First the kids. Ailsa flew through her A levels, turned down Oxbridge offers on the grounds that there were too many Bertie Wooster lookalikes at the open days she attended and went to Newcastle. First class honours and three years later, and a taste for Newcastle Brown, she's back in London training to be a lawyer. A proper job, a smart kid, we see each other a lot which usually involves a meal in London and far too much wine.

Cameron is second year at Leeds studying French and Politics. Remarkably he's avoided hard drugs and a life of crime which, when he was fifteen William Hill would have given you evens on. Oh, and he came home at the end of his first term declaring himself to be gay, which was absolutely fine by me. I think he was a bit surprised that I was so relaxed about it and that in itself made me a bit cross. 'Did you think I was homophobic then?' I asked him a few weeks after he'd made his announcement .

He said 'To be honest Dad, a bit'.

'Why?' I ask genuinely hurt

'Your language,' he says. 'You don't say 'poof' as such but some of your expressions ...'

'You have to remember Cam, the age I grew up in. Homosexuals on TV minced, were effeminate, and were to be laughed at. Probably some of that pretty ghastly culture did rub off on my generation.

But truly,' and I hug him as I say it, 'I don't mind who you fall in love with and who you shag ...'

'OK Dad, you can stop there, please...'

I continue, 'Who you shag and how as long as it's consensual, enjoyable and safe. OK?'

He looked at me and there were tears in his eyes.

'Stop crying you big girl's blouse,' I say and we both laugh.

So happy successful kids. Helen has left George. After I'd returned home from David's funeral, we'd met for coffee. I'd told her our shag-fest was over. I also exaggerated how much money Henry had cost me just to see the reaction. There wasn't one. Turned out she wasn't interested in my money, and she looked hurt when she realised that's what I'd thought of her.

We're friends now, we occasionally go out for meals so it's all very civilised, but utterly platonic. I think she's goes out on dates and that she wants a relationship, which is absolutely fine and dandy by me.

And Christine and I have remained friends. She's got a new man, a nice guy with a proper job of schoolteacher – younger and better-looking than me, so obviously I'm hurt by that ... And Christine teaches now too and seems utterly happy with her lot. Plus she has forgiven me for thinking she was a money-grabber too. So, all is settled in Jamie's domestic set-up .

Which then leaves Emily.

So, we did meet a few times. I went up to Scotland, she came down to London, but the theme of chastity ran through all our meetings. We made each other laugh constantly which was a good thing. I continued to find her sexually alluring and sometimes I felt that if I if kissed her she might respond positively. But I didn't and we never discussed taking things further.

And then she asked me to read her book. That's kind of an occupational hazard when you work in publishing, everyone assumes you're an expert on anything they've written regardless of genre. So, I've had manuscripts shoved through my letterbox on every bloody subject from bi-planes (can planes transition ...?) to histories of football clubs even more obscure than my own dear Heart of Midlothian.

But I said yes and she sent it to me electronically saying 'It's a novel of sorts. If you hate it, just tell me.'

I opened it and was transfixed by the second page, I read it in one go, in one sitting. What she'd written was funny, clever, sexy, pertinent and timely. It was political satire set in Scotland where the protagonist was a talented female politician, who couldn't get taken seriously because she was talented and female. Oh and as it happened, very attractive, She used her sexual wiles to destroy the men, and some women, who stopped her fulfilling her potential.

But it was also about power and privilege. Emily had interwoven the themes she'd talked about when we'd first met at the funeral. Four hundred folk owning half the Scottish countryside, polluting the hell out of it for profit and greed. She summed up perfectly stupidity of a nation whose people accept subjugation in the name of royalty, aristocracy privilege and obscene money-making.

I called her as soon as I had finished and told her I thought it was brilliant and must be published. She told me she'd sent it to 100 literary agents and had next to no response from any of them.

I told her I'd publish it.

Which I did, knowing damn all about publishing contemporary fiction but knowing some folk that did. Buying in expertise to promote the book through social media (whatever that is, it'll never catch on, trust me ...) the book took off.

I'm now publishing twenty-five books a year. I employ an office manager and a couple of editors and some sassy marketeers. Being a bit of an old hippy, every book that we consider commissioning has to be agreed upon by the majority of staff – but I do, being the benign dictator, have and often use a casting vote. We publish novels and works of non-fiction – to upset applecarts, the establishment and the status quo. We rail against the injustices and hypocrisy of this failing shabby nation.

We're basically a pain in the arse as a publishing house , hence our name, PITA Press.

I've put some money into the business which I am prepared to lose. I certainly won't put in any more as that smacks of the self-indulgence of the moderately wealthy. We won't publish something that we know won't at least breakeven, which means some interesting stuff does end up rejected. Staff and authors all share in any profits we do make, which on the publication of Emily's second novel (the first had TV rights sold on it) were quite healthy. I take out expenses only.

Emily is part of the submissions team. We speak often. She is now my best friend.

So Jamie the publishing philanthropist? Well, actually yes. I'm seemingly doing some good at last by bringing books to the market that I think make a real difference to people's lives. At the same time, I employ bright young people who will learn their trade and get well-rewarded for doing so. We've shabby, small overcrowded offices in the least fashionable part of south-east London, and I want everyone who works there to enjoy themselves and feel valued.

Do I sound smug? Maybe I am. But I'm smug and happy. I live in the present at last, I am fairly comfortable with what I have become, and who I am, which is a big difference to the Jamie you knew of yore. I have a vehicle through which to voice my dissatisfactions with the world around me, which saves me actually having to do it in person.

But fear not, I am not entirely modelling my new life on that of St Francis. I still like a drink, sometimes with my work colleagues, sometimes *tout seul*. But I do not cane it as of old. I have not had a cigarette since returning from David's funeral, I go to the gym three times a week and have learnt to swim if not exactly gracefully, just about in a straight line.

Lizzie's ghastly husband divorced her and installed a thirty-something-year-old replacement in the Cheshire mansion. Slighted thus, Lizzie secured a very generous settlement shortly before Geoffrey lost his tailored silk shirts on some property deal that went belly up in the Crash. Lizzie saw this as divine retribution and has become more or less sober, and certainly happy and optimistic. We meet every month for lunch, which invariably leads to something more. I won't put you off your supper by expanding on that allusion.,

It only leaves me to say thank you, Dear Reader – thank you for persevering with me. I know it can't have been easy, but my story is told. I am as close to being happy as anyone, I believe, can be. Jamie, the ranting, twisted, raging backward-looking man you have known is no more.

I wish you peace, love and understanding.

The End

David Grant is a writer and (non-fiction) publisher and lives in the South East of England. His first novel, *Elephant*, was published to critical acclaim in 2007.

This, the sequel, has taken rather longer to complete than he would like but this is because he is a self-acknowledged lazy bastard.

His comic thriller, *Nutshell*, will be published by Refreshing Words in 2025.

Printed in Great Britain
by Amazon

53021033R00155